ALSO BY

CARLO LUCARELLI

The Damned Season
Via delle Oche

CARTE BLANCHE

Carlo Lucarelli

CARTE BLANCHE

*Translated from the Italian
by Michael Reynolds*

editions

Europa Editions
116 East 16th Street
New York, N.Y. 10003
www.europaeditions.com
info@europaeditions.com

Translation by Michael Reynolds
Original title: *Carta bianca*
Translation copyright © 2006 by Europa Editions

Library of Congress Cataloging in Publication Data is available
ISBN 978-1-933372-15-0

Lucarelli, Carlo
Carte Blanche

Book design by Emanuele Ragnisco
www.mekkanografici.com

Printed in Canada

CONTENTS

PREFACE

I was supposed to graduate from Bologna University with a thesis in contemporary history on the police during the fascist period. I don't remember well what studies had brought me there, but I was collecting material for a thesis entitled "The Vision of the Police in the Memories of Anti-Fascists" when I ran across a strange character who in a certain sense changed my life.

He was a policeman who had spent forty years in the Italian police, from 1941 to 1981, when he retired. He had started in the fascist political police, the OVRA, a secret organization the meaning of whose very acronym was never known with certainty. As an "ovrino," he told me, his job was to tail, to spy on and to arrest anti-fascists who were plotting against the regime. Later, still as an ovrino, he was to tail, to spy on, and to arrest those fascists who disagreed with fascism's leader, Benito Mussolini. During the war, his job went back to tailing, spying on and arresting anti-fascist saboteurs, but towards the end of the war, when part of liberated Italy was under the control of partisan formations fighting alongside the Allies, my strange policeman friend actually became part of the partisan police. As he was good, he told me, he had never done anything particularly brutal and the partisans needed professionals like him to ensure public order and safety. Naturally, his duties included arresting fascists who had stained themselves with criminal acts during the war. Several years later, when, following elections, a regular government was formed in Italy, our policeman became part of the Italian Republic's police; his job, to tail, to spy on and to arrest some of those partisans who had been his colleagues and who were now considered dangerous subversives.

That encounter, and the studies I was undertaking at that moment, opened my eyes to a period fundamental in the history of Italy: strange, complicated and contradictory, as were the final years of the fascist regime in Italy.

Benito Mussolini and the fascists took power in October 1922. For twenty years, the regime consolidated itself into a ferocious dictatorship that suspended political and civil liberties, dissolved parties and newspapers, persecuted opponents and put practically all of Italy in uniform, like what was happening in the meantime in Hitler's Germany. The outbreak of World War II saw Italy allied with Nazi Germany, but a series of military defeats, the hostility of a people exhausted by the war effort, and the landing of the Anglo-American forces in Sicily in 1943 brought about the fall of the fascist regime. Mussolini was arrested and, on September 8, the new government decided to break the alliance with Hitler and carry on the war alongside the Allies.

At this point, Italy splits in two as the German army occupies that part of the country not yet liberated by the advance of the Anglo-American forces and puts Benito Mussolini in charge of a collaborationist government. This is one of the hardest and most ferocious moments in Italy's history. There is the war, stalled on the North Italian front, where there is fierce fighting, for at least a year. There is dread of the *Brigate Nere*, the Black Brigades, and the formations of the new fascist government's political police who, together with the German SS, repress sabotage activities and resistance by partisan formations. There is, above all, enormous moral and political confusion that mixes together the desperation of those who know they are losing, the opportunism of those ready to change sides, the guilelessness of those who haven't understood anything, and even the desire for revenge in those who are about to arrive.

Only a couple of years, until April 1945, when the war in Italy ends, but two ferocious, bloody, and above all confusing years, as I learned thanks to my studies and the accounts of my policeman friend. In Milan alone, for example, there were at least sixteen different police forces, from the regular police, the "Questura," to the Gestapo, each doing as they pleased and sometimes arresting one another.

But above all, I understood one thing from that encounter. For, after having heard that man recount forty years of his life in the Italian political police, during which with every change of government he found himself having to tail, to spy on, and to arrest those who had previously been his bosses, the question came spontaneously to me: "Excuse me, Marcsciallo, but . . . who do you vote for?" And he, with equal spontaneity, responded: "What does that have to do with it? I'm a policeman." As if to say: I don't take political stands. I do. I am a technician, a professional, not a politician.

At that point, I thought that there are moments in the life of a country in which the technicians and the professionals are also asked to account for their political choices and non-choices. I thought about what my policeman friend would have done if things had gone differently. And to ask oneself *what would have happened if* is the spring that triggers in your mind the idea for a novel.

So I started writing *Carte Blanche*. I invented Commissario De Luca, protagonist of two further novels in addition to *Carte Blanche*, *The Damned Season* and *Via delle Oche*, and lost myself in his adventures.

And I never did write my thesis.

Carlo Lucarelli

Officers and agents of the public security forces are entrusted with the safeguard of citizens' welfare and the preservation of public order, the protection of persons and of properties, and, in general, the prevention of crime; they gather evidence of these crimes, and proceed, in accordance with the law, to the identification and arrest of delinquents.

(Art. 1, Consolidated Act
of Public Safety Laws, 1931)

– The Republic must end well. Even if the government falls, it must take into consideration the fascists who remain behind. Larice, how dependable are the Polizia?
– Not very, Duce.
– I knew it . . .

(Conversation between Benito Mussolini
and Settimio Larice, Chief-of-police,
24 April 1945)

CHAPTER ONE

The bomb exploded suddenly, with a ferocious blast, right as the funeral procession was crossing the street. De Luca threw himself to the ground, instinctively, and covered his head with his hands as a section of wall collapsed onto the sidewalk, showering him in dust. Everybody started shouting. A sergeant from the Republican National Guard stretched a machine gun out over De Luca's body and fired an endless burst that deafened him and brought a deluge of broken pantiles down onto the street.

"Bastards," the sergeant cried. "Sons of bitches!"

"Bastardi!" everybody cried, all of them shooting: the GNR, the Black Brigades, the Decima Mas marines, the police. All of them except De Luca, on the ground with his face in the dust, his hands open on his head, his fingers stuck in his hair. He remained like that for an interminable moment, and only when everybody had stopped shooting and all that could be heard were the moans of the injured, only then did he lift himself to his knees, brushing the dust off his trench coat, and get back to his feet.

"They'll pay for this!" a striper cried into his face, grabbing him by the lapels of his coat. "Retaliation! Carte blanche!"

"Carte blanche, right," said De Luca, freeing himself from the hysterical grip that was stripping him of his clothes. "Sure, sure."

He moved away quickly, without turning back, sighing through lips that tasted of dust. His knee hurt. Knew I shouldn't have stopped to watch, he thought, and turned the corner as the first trucks stopped with a screech of brakes and the Germans leapt out to close off the streets.

De Luca threw his hands deep into his pockets and pulled his trench coat tight as spring was late arriving that year and it was still cold. He turned another corner and counted down the building numbers to fifteen. He mounted the first step, went back to check the number again—via Battisti, 15—then entered resolutely. He passed by an elevator with its cage and commanding wrought-iron gate and stopped in front of the porter's window, but there was nobody in. He started up a flight of stairs—white and exceptionally clean, like marble. A high-class building. And for contrast's sake, running his hand over his stubbly chin, he thought it was time to get himself a shave. On the first floor, a man came towards him; he was big, he wore a heavy overcoat and had a square policeman's face.

"What happened?" asked the man, alarmed. "That noise outside . . . "

"An attack," De Luca said. "They threw a bomb at Tornago's funeral. But everything's under control now."

"Ah, okay." The man shook his head, as if he were about to say something else, but then took a step forward and planted a hand against De Luca's chest as he made for the door, stopping him mid-stride with his leg out and a counterblow that hurt his neck.

"Hey there, friend! Where do you think you're going?"

De Luca closed his eyes, momentarily ironing out the creases that insomnia had etched on his face. He made a sign with his right hand as if to say "just a second," and with his left hand pulled a badge out of his pocket that the gorilla, turning white, recognized immediately, even before reading it. He stretched out his arm in salute, clicking his heels.

"Excuse me, Comandante. If you had told me at once . . . "

De Luca nodded and put away his badge.

"No harm done," he said, "but don't call me Comandante, I'm not with the Brigata Muti anymore. I'm with the police. This is my case. Who's inside?"

"Maresciallo Pugliese, from the Mobile Squad. And the team."

"No authorities? Journalists? Family?"

"Only the police."

"Good. Don't let anybody in . . . except me, that is. Let me through, please."

"Sorry. At your command, Comandante."

"Commissario, not Comandante. Commissario."

"Yes, sorry, sir. At your command, Commissario."

De Luca sighed as the gorilla moved to one side and opened the door. He entered a vestibule that was rather narrow, small, quite different to how he had imagined it. To one side of the entrance there was a white telephone sitting on a small, bow-legged side-table, on the other side a hat tree and several prints on the wall; at the far end, in a part of the room framed by the doorway, as if in a painting, there were two men. They watched De Luca as he approached. One was short with a bird's beak nose and a black hat, the other young, thin, wearing glasses.

"What happened?" asked the short one in a heavy southern accent. "A bomb?"

"An attack," De Luca repeated. "Grenades at Tornago's funeral."

"Only grenades?" said the thin fellow. "Sounded like the front had shifted here."

"They lost their heads and started shooting, all of them."

The thin one took off his glasses, shaking his head as he did so. "Someone'll have gotten killed, no doubt. They're in such bad shape that they're killing themselves. Even a funeral has become dangerous, even the funeral of an impor—" He stopped, because the short one, who was looking hard at De Luca with narrowed eyes, had squeezed his arm just above the elbow.

"Why, I know you, don't I?" he said, as De Luca got closer. "You're part of the Political Police. Is this your case, then? We're more than happy to hand it over to you. C'mon, Albertini, let's go."

De Luca held up his hand, stopping them at the doorstep with a deep sigh that was almost a groan.

"How many times must I repeat it today?" he said. "I'm not with the Political Police anymore, I'm Commissario De Luca, assigned to the police. They transferred me yesterday from the Brigata Ettore Muti, special division of the Political Police, and I don't have my papers yet, but we work together. They gave me this case. That okay?"

The beak-nosed man took his hat off, bowing his head. "At your command," he said. Albertini, on the other hand, didn't utter another word.

De Luca entered the room. There next to him, to his right, a man was lying face up on the floor against the wall, his arm bent upwards. He was dressed in a powder-blue silk dressing gown and he had a large, dark, sticky wound in his chest right over his heart. Another wound, in the groin, was partly visible under the bloodied flap of his dressing gown. De Luca looked at him at length, then let his gaze drift: the walls plastered with books, the writing desk with the glass lamp, the armchairs in the middle of the room, the coffee table, the chandelier, the mirrors, the rug, everything neat and tidy. It was a rich man's building, all right.

"Who is he?" De Luca asked, turning back to the corpse.

"Name's Rehinard," said the short man. Albertini had stopped talking altogether.

"German?"

"He was from Trento. Italian citizen."

"You know him?"

"No, I've got his wallet. Here."

From the entrance came a noise, but De Luca didn't turn.

"It's one of my men going through the other rooms," said the short man. "It's a big apartment, four rooms, the bathroom, the kitchen, and nobody in it but him. So, do you want this wallet?"

De Luca took the wallet of heavy, hand-tooled crocodile leather, and walked over to the coffee table in the middle of the room. He sat down in an armchair and emptied the wallet's contents onto the glass top beside two empty glasses. He noticed the rim of one was stained with lipstick.

"Papers," said the short man, as De Luca examined them. "Party membership card, money, and some visiting cards." One was most elegant, embossed in ornate lettering that read *Count Alberto Maria Tedesco,* and another more simple, smooth, with *Sibilla* written in italics and a telephone number. De Luca held the Count's card in his hand, as if weighing it, then dropped it down with the others.

"Where's the maid?"

"Excuse me?"

"The maid, the servant, the cleaning woman, what do you call her?"

The short man looked at De Luca strangely, frowning over his thin eyes. "There is no maid," he said.

"In a home this clean and tidy? A single man, a bachelor, according to the documents?" De Luca stood up and wandered around the room. "Seems too tidy to me for an hourly maid, unless she just left. Or maybe it's a manservant. One of the rooms may be his, his stuff'll be in it. Isn't there anything down at the station on this guy that you know of?"

"Not as far as I remember, and I remember everything. It's more likely that you have something on him. I mean . . . "

"As a matter of fact, there is, but not much." De Luca remembered the yellow record: Rehinard Vittorio, member of the PFR, the Fascist Republican Party, and that was it. He remembered it precisely for this reason. "The doctor been yet?" he asked.

"Not yet, but we've called him."

"And Maresciallo Pugliese?"

"That's me. Pugliese."

"Oh."

De Luca stopped again in front of the corpse. He looked at it, then moved aside the edge of the dressing gown covering his legs with the point of his shoe. Albertini turned away. Pugliese, instead, came closer, leaning forward, his hands on his knees.

"Jealousy?" he said. De Luca shrugged.

"Maybe," he mumbled. "A woman was here, and not long ago. I'd say a blond, judging from the color of the lipstick on that glass. There's no weapon, right?"

"No, we haven't found it yet, be it a stiletto or a knife."

"A paper knife."

"A paper knife?" Pugliese shot him another sidelong glance.

"Might very well be. It's the only thing missing from the writing desk, which really does have everything, and there are a couple of opened envelopes with today's date." De Luca went back to the coffee table and fell into an armchair. He drew his face to the lipstick-stained glass and gave it a keen sniff. Alcohol. At that hour of the morning? Strange. The other was empty. Suddenly, as had repeatedly been the case over the past week, a wave of sleep washed over him, making him yawn; always at the wrong time, never at night, when he would lie awake in bed watching the darkness on the ceiling, or tossing and turning, eyelids clamped shut, twisted up in his bed sheet.

"Who called you?" he asked.

"The porter," said Pugliese. "The one who discovered the

body. He was passing by and saw the door wide open. He came in and saw everything. His wife telephoned us."

A balding man wearing lightweight spectacles came into the room and stopped, looking first at De Luca and then at Pugliese, who returned his look with a nod.

"Nothing there," said the bald man. "Only the bathroom and one of the rooms look lived in, the others are empty."

"No other room? I don't know, women's stuff in the closet? Things like that?" De Luca asked, and Pugliese smiled when the bald man shook his head.

"Nothing. Only a bedroom with a man's belongings: clothes, toiletries, shoes . . . "

"Bed soiled?"

"Sorry?"

"Physiological marks on the sheets?"

"Oh, right. No, nothing. Everything in its place, even the bed is made."

"Hair in the brush?"

The bald man, annoyed, glanced at Pugliese. "Blond, straight, long, like on the head of the gentleman there."

De Luca nodded, collapsing back into the armchair. His head sank down between his shoulders, sagging down into the collar of his trench coat. He stretched his legs out, digging his heels into the floor, and he could have fallen asleep there and then; enveloped in a cloud of white, dusty fabric cut in two by his black shirt, his face wrinkled and unshaven slumping slowly towards his chest.

"Are you feeling all right?" said Pugliese. "You look rotten."

"Insomnia," murmured De Luca, "And not only that . . . but, don't worry, I'm not about to fall asleep. I was just thinking. We just have to talk to the porter and find out what kind of character this Rehinard was, who he saw and who was here this morning. And if he had a maid, because as far as I'm concerned something doesn't add up here."

Pugliese nodded vigorously. "Fine. And then?"

De Luca looked him straight in the eyes, serious. "And then, nothing. What more do you want to do? We have a rather well-off stiff on our hands, a party-member connected to Tedesco. You know Tedesco, right? Minister for Foreign Affairs . . . Look at how he's been killed: this promises to be a dirty case. Do you think an investigation is going to be possible? Or that anybody cares, at a moment like this, with the Americans almost to Bologna? I'll cut my own throat if they let us continue."

Pugliese smiled and opened his arms widely as De Luca put his hands on the armrests and in a sudden movement got to his feet, unsteadily.

"At your command," said Pugliese as he followed him to the door with his hat in hand. He stopped in front of the elevator, his finger nearly on the call button, but then hurried off on his short legs to catch up with De Luca, who was already halfway down the first flight of stairs.

"Comandante!" he wheezed. "Damn it! Sorry, Commissa, I can't seem to remember! Listen, Commissario, if you don't mind, when we're with the porter let me show him my badge. If they see yours, they'll scare and they won't talk at all."

De Luca didn't reply. They reached the porter's room and Pugliese rapped on the glass with his knuckles, but De Luca opened the door and went straight in, assailed by the stink of cooked cabbage and stale air that wrinkled his nose and turned his stomach. Inside, there was a gray-haired woman sitting on a wicker chair in front of a lighted stove with a rosary in her hand. She gave the impression of looking older than she was.

"Good morning," said De Luca, addressing the old woman, who looked at him with her mouth open. "I'm trying to find the porter."

Pugliese entered and pulled aside a curtain that separated

the room from the rest of the apartment. A cabbage pot was boiling on a range.

"I don't know anything," said the old woman. "My husband's out and I don't know anything."

"But you know the gentleman upstairs, don't you?" De Luca asked. The old woman shrugged.

"I'm not the one who knows everybody," she said. "That's my husband."

"Well, to look at him he seemed like a nice person, that man," said Pugliese wheedlingly. The old woman turned toward Pugliese with a start, making the rosary beads tinkle.

"A nice person? With all the women visitors he received up there at all hours? Don't know much about people, do you?"

"What does receiving some nice girls mean nowadays . . . "

"These days there are no nice girls. It's the war's fault. Just this morning there were two of them here, one was that blonde, a pretty girl but crazy as a loon, and strange, a Count's daughter, my husband said . . . And the other one, a brunette with glasses, another strange one . . . But I don't know anything. Every now and again I see something from in here, because I'm old and I've got a pain in my legs that . . . "

"Fine," De Luca said brusquely, cutting the woman short, and behind his back Pugliese shook his head. "Besides the two ladies, did you see anyone else go up this morning?"

"No, my husband, maybe . . . "

"Okay, we get the idea. Where is your husband?"

"After the police arrived," she said pointing at Pugliese, "he went out on an errand." De Luca looked at Pugliese, who shrugged.

"He'll be back," he said.

"Let's hope so," said De Luca. He turned and started towards the door, but the old woman stopped him, beginning to speak again.

"A nice person!" she said bitterly. "With all the misery

that's around these days, bread that's up to fifteen lire a kilo, when you can find it that is, and him throwing money away! Who can say where it come from . . . and he was also getting about with the Germans!"

"Germans?" asked Pugliese. He glanced at De Luca, who was looking at the old woman.

"That's right. My husband told me, because I'm no expert when it comes to these things, but there was this soldier who'd visit, an officer, and he had red flashes on his collar, with those . . . " With a sharpened nail at the end of a thin finger she traced two parallel marks in the air and Pugliese turned aside with a grimace.

"That's done it," he said. "The SS."

"Even better," said De Luca. "At least we'll be through quickly. Tell me something else: did that gentleman have a maid? A servant?"

"Oh yes. Assuntina." De Luca allowed himself the shadow of a tired smile. "From down South, she was, an evacuee. She was permanent there with him, though if you ask me, things like that are not right . . . But she left three days ago."

De Luca turned once more and this time nobody stopped him. He left the porter's room, and Pugliese hopped along behind him to the front steps. Outside a GNR patrol was stopping people, their machine guns in full view. A man in civilian clothes who was checking papers greeted De Luca, who didn't respond.

"What now?" Pugliese asked, putting on his hat. He seemed shorter with the hat.

"We have to report back to the chief of police. We tell them that a questionable character, a Party member, a friend of the SS as well as of Count Tedesco's daughter—whose father, by the way, is no less than a member of the Republic's diplomatic corps and a personal friend of Marshall Graziani—has been killed and castrated by who knows who, with a weapon that has gone missing. If only it had been the poor, jealous maid; she has been missing for three days, no less, from a home in which the beds were made this morning. We know this thanks to the information given us by a porter who this morning most helpfully decided to run an errand, despite the police and a dead body upstairs. What do you think the Chief will say?"

"What will the Chief say?" Pugliese repeated with a wry smile.

"What I'm about to say now." De Luca pulled his badge out from inside his trench coat and opened it before a militiaman who was heading towards them with a menacing look. "Out of my fucking way, son," he said. "This here is none of your business. Just forget it."

CHAPTER TWO

"Forget it? You're mad, De Luca, what are you saying?"

The Chief got up out of the armchair and came out from behind his desk, planting himself in front of De Luca, who was sitting uncomfortably in a wooden chair as stiff as an accused man, his arms folded across his chest, looking at the floor.

"Listen, there's been a crime, a serious crime at that, and we can't simply forget about it. You went to great lengths to get yourself transferred to the police, and now you come up with crap like this. It's not like you."

De Luca didn't say anything, keeping his eyes fixed on the floor. Behind him, slouched in an armchair, with one leg over an armrest, lazily dangling a shiny boot, was Federale Vitali, Party Secretary, who watched him in silence, a tight smile on his thin lips.

The Chief went back behind his desk, but didn't sit; he remained standing, authoritative, hands in waistcoat pockets, at the top of the curve of his rotund belly, right beneath the pugnacious jaw of Il Duce hanging on the wall.

"If something is scaring you," he said paternally. "If someone is putting pressure on you, or seeking to prevent justice from coming out into the open, it is our duty to—"

"It is Il Duce's express will," Vitali said without getting up, "and ours, too, obviously, that the police carry out their duties without impediments, for those matters within their jurisdiction. Why, the police must arrest thieves and murderers so that the Italian people know that in fascist Italy, even in difficult times, the law is always the law! Over here things are not as they are in the South, where scum and Badoglians treat the law like their plaything . . . An important case like this must serve to show people that the police force is present and watchful!"

The Chief gestured with his hand, nodding solemnly, as if to say that those were his words. He sat in the armchair, which squeaked under his weight.

"Just to be clear," said De Luca. "What is it you want me to do?"

The Chief smiled. "You're one of the best police investigators around; you were before going to the Brigata Muti, and you are now. Investigate. Find the murderer."

"In complete confidence, of course . . . "

"On the contrary, Commissario." With a rustle of his black fascist uniform Vitali got up and stood behind De Luca, making his boots creak. "On the contrary: You will be furnished with generous space in the papers and all means will be at your disposal. Full support from the Party."

He too walked around the desk and stopped beside the Chief. He was a small, edgy-looking man, with raven hair that was swept back and plastered down with grease. De Luca looked at them at length, in silence, and then nodded.

"I understand," he said. "I find Rehinard's murderer. Then?"

"Then you arrest him. Handcuff him and take him to jail. Isn't this your job?"

"Even if it's a Count?"

"Even if it's a Count."

"Even if it's a German?"

Vitali grimaced, stretching his thin lips. "Of course, a German, no. But that is obvious."

"Obvious," echoed the Chief. "Good, that's enough chatter, go to work. You're on this case only; you'll be supplied with a car and all the men you want. The Federale has put the Milizia on hand for whatever help may be needed."

Vitali clicked his shiny new heels with a loud snap, bowing his head, and then tensed.

"Commissario De Luca," he cried. "Fascist Italy is watching you! Saluto al Duce!"

Albertini was standing in the street before the building's door. His eyes shot open when he saw De Luca arrive in a car accompanied by a truck full of militiamen that climbed onto the sidewalk and stopped with a metallic lament from the brakes. De Luca got out and signaled to a striper, who came over running.

"Has the doctor been over already?" he asked Albertini.

"Already been and gone. He spoke with the Maresciallo."

"Good. Paper knife turn up?"

"Paper knife? Oh, the murder weapon. No, no sign of it. Excuse me, Commissario, but who are they?"

"They're here to help," said De Luca. "Complete cooperation." He pointed out the door to the sergeant. "Turn the place upside down and bring me that weapon; if you don't find it in the house, look in the street. I want it by tonight. Is Pugliese still upstairs?"

"Well, no, I was waiting here to tell you. Pugliese is expecting you at Rosina's."

"At Rosina's?"

Albertini smiled. "It's a trattoria, right across the street, right there, see? Come on, I'll walk you over."

They crossed the street and, parting a greasy-looking rattan curtain, entered. Inside there were a few tables covered with checkered tablecloths, a chrome counter, and a suffocating odor of frying. The tables were all occupied, and at one in the corner, Pugliese was sitting in front of a glass of red wine. He stood when he saw De Luca and pulled out a chair for him, pouring some wine into an empty glass.

"Come, Commissario, I was waiting for you."

"What are you doing here?" asked De Luca sternly.

"It's noon and you've got to eat if you want to work, right? The food's good here, it's cheap and there's even a telephone that works. Trust me, Commissario, I've been here seven years and I've always done all my work from here."

De Luca hesitated, then shrugged and sat down. "These are not my preferred methods," he muttered as Pugliese pushed the glass in his direction.

"I know all about you, I do," said Pugliese as he signaled to Albertini to sit down. "You're the type that never relaxes, always tense . . . You remind me of poor Commissario Lenzi, bright, efficient, but what an ulcer!"

De Luca picked up his glass, looking at the traces left by the red wine. "What happened to him? I mean, this Lenzi, did he die of ulcer?"

Pugliese sighed and gestured to a waitress to bring Albertini a glass. "He was confused," said Pugliese. "A good man, but confused . . . After Italy's collapse on September 8, he made some mistakes and ended up against a wall. Germans."

De Luca nodded. "I see," he said quietly. "But I don't really think I'm like him. I'm a policeman."

The girl arrived with a glass and as she walked away, Albertini turned to gaze at her backside. Pugliese even leaned forward.

"This is another reason why I like Rosina's," he said, but it seemed as though De Luca's thoughts were elsewhere.

"Is the porter back?" he asked.

Albertini shook his head. "No sign of him," he said. "And his wife is starting to get worried. She says that since they were married, the only time he didn't come back before noon was when the army recalled him in 1917 after the battle of Caporetto."

"He must be searched for."

Pugliese frowned. "Why? What did the Chief tell you?"

"He told me to find Rehinard's murderer."

"Strange."

"It's our job."

"Of course, but . . . I mean . . . For fuck's sake, Commissa, you know exactly what I mean!"

"I know, and it is indeed strange. And as I see it, also dangerous. They want something to distract people, but I don't trust that snake Vitali at all. The press is going to be all over us, too."

"Christ, even get our names in the papers! Well, that's just great."

The waitress came back with two plates of spaghetti, put one down in front of De Luca, and passed the other to Pugliese, then left, dragging her slippers, followed by Albertini's gaze.

"I ordered for you, too, Commissa. If you don't want it, I'll send it back."

De Luca shook his head. He hadn't eaten breakfast, but, as usual, the minute he sat down at a table his appetite left him, like sleep at night, only to come back when it was most inopportune. At that moment, he even felt nauseous. He picked up the plate and passed it to Albertini, who thanked him with a nod, then took off his trench coat and laid it on the chair next to him, carefully, as his pistol was in the pocket. He took a sip of red wine and waited with a grimace for the heartburn to arrive, then obstinately drank another.

"The porter must be searched for," he said.

Pugliese sighed, winding an enormous knot of spaghetti onto his fork.

"What a bad habit, Commissario."

"Strange that he should go missing like this," De Luca continued. "I don't like it. Then, we've got to find this little cleaning girl. We'll have to pass by Party headquarters to get information on this Rehinard."

Albertini let a smile slip, hiding it behind his napkin. "Will you be going, Commissario? Because if I show up there asking things like that they'll be kicking me out."

"We've got carte blanche, haven't we? Full support, so Vitali said . . . and if they don't collaborate, well, even better, we'll be finished sooner. What did the doctor say?"

Pugliese looked pleadingly at De Luca, who, with closed eyes, was sipping more wine.

"Do you have to know right this minute? Okay, fine . . . At a rough guess, based on a preliminary examination, Rehinard's death was caused by a stab with a sharp weapon, rather precise, that killed him instantly. The second stab, to the genitals, was inflicted later and was superfluous. He must have died not more than four or five hours ago, some time this morning, that is. Doctor Martini always hits the mark when it comes to time of death. In a couple of days he ought to be able to tell you more. Why don't you eat something instead of drinking all that wine on an empty stomach? Maybe you'd prefer to eat something plain, spaghetti without sauce?"

De Luca held his hand up, staring at the glass.

"As soon as you've finished," he said to Albertini, "run over to PFR headquarters to ask about Rehinard, Commissario De Luca's request, Vitali's orders. Then phone the station and issue an arrest warrant for, what's the porter's name?"

"Galimberti, Oreste Galimberti."

"For him, okay? Get it out to the police precincts, division headquarters, GNR, the Political Police, everywhere, even the Muti."

Albertini gulped down the last of his wine, cast a final glance at the passing waitress's backside and left.

"Who can be trusted in the squad?" asked De Luca after a while. Pugliese poured him some more wine, seeing him hold out his glass.

"All of them, Commissario," responded Pugliese. "They're all good men and earnest patriots."

"That's not what I mean. Something's not right here, Pugliese."

"Oh, well, if you mean smart, tactful guys who'll show some discretion, then there's Albertini—though he's a bit of a hothead—and Ingangaro, the bald fellow you saw this morning. Also Marcon, the guard at the door; he isn't too bright, but he knows how to do his job."

"Good." De Luca looked at the reddish shadow tinging the glass from which he had drunk. "Put Ingangaro on that maid, get him to run a check on evacuees and to go through every floor of the building asking about Rehinard."

"Will do. And us? What'll we do? Shall we have a real coffee?"

"Without a doubt. Then we'll call Tedesco and get ourselves an appointment for today. Wait a second: how is it they've got real coffee in this place?"

"Good heavens, Commissario, don't you ever relax? Finish your wine and let me take care of that, don't you worry about it . . . "

CHAPTER THREE

"Yes?"

"Commissario De Luca and Maresciallo Pugliese. Police. We have an appointment with the Count."

"One moment." The woman pulled her head back inside, closing the door. De Luca wrapped the collar of his trench coat around his neck and lifted his eyes to the silent façade of the building towering over them. A second later the door reopened, revealing an old man.

"Yes?"

"Commissario De Luca and Maresciallo Pugliese, police. We'd like to see the Count. We have an appointment."

The old man opened the door wide and stood aside to let them in. They entered an enormous hall with a big staircase. Suddenly the old man said, "One moment," and disappeared. De Luca clenched his teeth.

"Now I'm really starting to get pissed off," he muttered. Pugliese grinned. They waited in a convent-like gloomy half-light; one minute, two minutes, almost a third, then the sharp sound of far-off footsteps resounded in the total, almost surreal silence that filled the building and a young priest entered through one of the doors. It really felt like being in a convent. The priest came towards them briskly, his frock swinging to and fro around his ankles and across his black patent leather shoes.

"Yes?" he asked.

"Police. Commissario De Luca and Maresciallo Pugliese. We want to see the Count."

The priest nodded, as if meditating, his gaze lowered. The short beard framing his thin face and a pair of glasses did nothing to make him seem any older. "Of course, of course," he mumbled and then lifted his eyes to De Luca. "May I know the reason for your visit? I'm Don Vincenzo Peroni, private secretary to His Excellence the Count, who is very, very busy."

"As I explained over the telephone," De Luca said, "it's about a homicide. One of the Count's collaborators has been murdered and we would like to have some information on him and on relations between the two. His name was Vittorio Rehinard."

Don Vincenzo nodded again, his eyes lowered. He seemed to meditate on every word that came his way.

"Signor Rehinard no longer collaborates with His Excellence and hasn't for the past fifteen days. And he stopped coming to this house at least a month ago. As I'm sure you know, signor Rehinard was responsible for relationships between His Excellence's offices and the Holy See. A capable collaborator, but recently he had been complaining of health problems and was planning to retire."

"Very interesting," said De Luca. That slow, smooth voice pushing every word down deep was starting to grate on him. "But I'd like to hear it from the Count himself."

I'd . . . like . . . to . . . Don Vincenzo nodded at every word.

"His Excellence is genuinely sorry that he agreed to an appointment which unfortunately he cannot keep. Unexpected business, you understand, of national interest . . . " he said, and placed his finger in front of his mouth, nodding gravely. De Luca lifted his eyes to the ceiling and Pugliese was certain he read a profanity on his lips. Don Vincenzo saw it too, with his clear, impassive eyes.

"I don't care a damn about His Excellence's unexpected business!" he growled with an I-don't-care-a-damn that seemed as if it had come straight out of one of Mussolini's speeches. "This is an official police investigation, a case of murder! If his lordship the Count doesn't want to speak with us, I'll have him summoned to the station tomorrow morning!"

Don Vincenzo started, more than he had for the profanity, and stopped nodding. "You have no idea what you're saying! A police station! Impossible! But if you insist, I will see what can be done. Perhaps His Excellence will receive you . . . or he may be able to explain himself better than I." He uttered these last words in the same soft tones, nonetheless they seemed a threat. He turned with a sudden flourish, the frock wrapping around his legs. When it fell back in place, he stepped forward, inviting them to follow him. He opened a door and stepped to one side, showing them into what appeared to be a library.

"Please wait here," he said, then closed the door, his rapid footsteps echoing down the hall.

"Christ almighty," snarled De Luca. "I will have him brought to the station, in uniformed company, too!"

"Forget it, Commissa. Back there already, with that priest . . . You'll end up making a false step."

"Great! Then they'd take me off this case. I ask for nothing more, Pugliese."

"Forget about it. Have a look at this stuff instead." Pugliese cast a glance around, pointing his hat at the walls covered with bookshelves. The room was large, divided in two by an enormous divan, facing away from the two men. The light that came in through a window covered by a heavy curtain wasn't a lot. Pugliese walked over to the books, squinting so as to read the titles.

"Great fun," he said. "*Education for Death, The Martyrdom*

of St. Sebastian, The Science of the Cross . . . Have a look at that painting there—Agh! Jesus!"

Pugliese, proceeding alongside the bookshelves, had started and dropped his hat. He was staring at the divan and De Luca moved to come in front of it. He too froze, dumbfounded. Sitting on the divan, immobile, her eyes two slits and her legs crossed, was a girl. She held her arms at her sides, inert, the palms of her hands face up, and her short dress had slipped up over her knees. She was blond, with a pageboy haircut and a fringe over her forehead, very pretty, diminutive, and pallid. She was missing one shoe. De Luca watched her breast for a second to see if she was breathing, then saw it moving, slowly. He thought she was asleep, but her lips parted.

"You're disturbing me," she murmured.

"Sorry?" said Pugliese.

"You're bothering me. Please go away and leave me alone."

De Luca moved closer, leaning forward to see better those slightly bulging eyes of hers hidden behind their drooping eyelids and noted her red lips, an intense red. Like that on the glass.

"We're waiting for the Count," he said. "They showed us in here, we had no idea there was somebody else. We . . . "

The girl opened her eyes, looked at De Luca and then, without shifting, turned her head towards Pugliese. She had green eyes, a dull green, and a strange, soft look, like someone who's just woken up or is on the edge of drunkenness.

"I like sitting all alone in the dark with my thoughts," she said. "It relaxes me and I nearly fall asleep. Have you ever done it?"

"Oh sure," said Pugliese, after having glanced at De Luca. "Very often. It's a great pastime."

"Sit down here beside me, please." The girl patted the divan's heavy velour. "Where is my shoe?"

Pugliese looked around and saw the toe of a black shoe poking out from under the curtain. He picked it up and sat down, with a moment of embarrassment, but she took the shoe from him and held it in her hand. De Luca leaned back against the mantelpiece in front of her.

"Are you Sonia Tedesco, the Count's daughter?"

"And who are you?"

"Commissario De Luca."

"Are you here to arrest me?"

"Have you done something wrong?" asked Pugliese. She shrugged. Her dress was black, summery and quite tight, open at the neck and shoulders but with long sleeves.

"Do you know Vittorio Rehinard?" asked De Luca. She lifted her face to look at him from under her eyelids.

"I don't like you." She turned to Pugliese and touched the tip of his nose with her fingertip, a tiny finger with a rounded nail. Pugliese blushed. "You, on the other hand, I do like. I'll tell you. Yes, I knew Signor Rehinard."

"Had you known him for a long time?"

"For as long as my father has known him."

"When did you last see him?"

"Perhaps when he came here last Friday."

"Didn't you go to his apartment this morning?"

"I never get up before noon."

Sonia Tedesco stretched her leg out towards De Luca, handing him her shoe, without looking at him. "Would you mind putting on my shoe?" she asked. "My foot is cold."

"With pleasure," said De Luca with a sigh and a quick glance at Pugliese, who was smiling widely. He leaned over and, holding her by the ankle, delicately slipped the shoe onto her foot, so she quickly lifted her leg and touched him with her toe, brushing against him lightly, inside his trench coat just below his belt; a rapid movement that escaped Pugliese.

"What kind of man is this Rehinard?" asked Pugliese, as De Luca, surprised and embarrassed, watched Sonia, impassive, and asked himself if she really had done it on purpose.

"Handsome," said Sonia. "Very handsome. But also very stupid. Everybody liked him."

"Did you like him too?"

Sonia shrugged again. "Everybody liked him, even Valeria."

"Who's Valeria?" asked De Luca, but just then the library door opened and a man entered. He was tall and had a head of wild, thick, graying hair with one unruly curl falling over his corrugated brow.

"I am extremely annoyed . . . " he began, calmly, then he took a step forward and at once saw Sonia sitting on the divan. "What are you doing here?" he hissed, his voice trembling. "These are not things that concern women. Leave us alone this minute!"

Sonia got up without saying a word, the shadow of a smile on her lips, blowing a maverick lock of hair off her forehead. With languid, rolling steps that stretched her dress tight over her thighs, she moved away, and when she passed by De Luca, something brushed against his trench coat, at the height of his crotch: a light, fleeting touch that was, however, enough to make him recoil instinctively against the wall. To hide his embarrassment, he coughed into the cavity of his closed hand. As soon as Sonia had left, the Count went on the offensive.

"This is unacceptable!" he cried, slamming his fist down on the desk. "I am a personal friend of Il Duce and I deserve some respect! I will not allow two lackeys with badges to treat me as if I were a delinquent."

"Signor Count, perhaps we . . . " De Luca began, but the Count cut him short.

"Isn't a police officer required to shave? What kind of example are you setting for your subordinates? Get out of here this minute!" He opened the library door and held it wide open. De Luca began to shake, but not with fear. An icy rage was making him quiver from his toes to the hairs on his head.

"We'll leave at once," he said. "But I wish to inform you that tomorrow morning you are ordered to appear at precinct headquarters for questioning. I will send two officers and, if necessary, you'll be brought in handcuffed. Good morning." And he walked out, clenching fists and teeth, followed by Pugliese and the furious voice of the Count.

"I'll make a phone call that will put you in your place, copper. You'll see!"

Outside the sky was turning gray and the air bore a wet, metallic smell of rain. De Luca walked towards the car, pulling his trench coat tight around himself and shoving his hands ever deeper into the pockets of his coat as Pugliese ran after him. He didn't say a word until he was seated, and then he slammed his fist down on the dash like a hammer.

"They were all playing us for fools, beginning with that priest," he growled. "But I'll have them all locked up, and then I'll have them spitting up blood!"

Pugliese started the car with some difficulty as it was a handsome official vehicle, but far from new.

"Forget about it, Commissa," he said, dropping the car off the sidewalk. "With the way you stirred things up in there, tomorrow they'll take the case from you and put you on passports."

"I wish!"

Pugliese shook his head. "You don't really mean that. I'm starting to understand you, I am. You're the type of person who's got to finish what he starts, who gets mad as hell if something doesn't add up, particularly if people try to hide things from him. What do you think of little Sonia?"

De Luca shifted in his seat; the idea of her perturbed him, though he didn't want it to, and he had other things to think of. "The same as you, no doubt: eyes dull, reflexes sluggish, pale, and that tone of voice. Morphine?"

"Definitely. I would like to have seen her arms."

"And what was that about last Friday? Why did that priest tell me that they hadn't seen Rehinard for a month if he was in that house last Friday? And why did Sonia tell me that she never gets up before noon when she was at Rehinard's early this morning? She's the blonde the portress saw. And who is this Valeria? You're right Pugliese: this case interests me. It smells fishy, but it interests me."

"I'm glad. What do we do now?"

"Back to via Battisti. I want to talk to that old woman in the building before going any further."

The GNR truck was still parked on the sidewalk. A striper was sitting on the footboard smoking, his hands resting against the machine gun hanging from his neck. Nearby, Albertini and Marcon were talking; on seeing the car arrive they hurried over. Marcon opened De Luca's door, holding it by the handle, while Albertini turned to Pugliese.

"They're still looking for the weapon," he said. "It can't be found anywhere. We've searched the apartment from top to bottom, and a whole lot of things have turned up: an address book full of addresses of big names, photographs of this Rehinard fellow at all ages." It was obvious that he was about to say something important, a smile quivered in the corner of his mouth.

"C'mon, Albertini," said Pugliese. "What is it?"

Albertini grinned. He put his hand in a pocket of his overcoat and pulled out a parcel wrapped in newspaper opened at one end.

"Look at this, Maresciallo. It was under the bed, tied to a leg. I found it by chance with all that mess the GNR made. Some help they are! It's morphine."

"Shit!" said Pugliese, taking the packet and weighing it in his hand. "Decent amount, too. So that's what our Rehinard was up to."

"Very interesting," said De Luca thoughtfully, leaning up against the automobile. "Very interesting. This is yet another link between Rehinard and Sonia Tedesco. Where might he have gotten it from?"

"I had a look inside," said Albertini, still talking to Pugliese. "Some of the packets are unmarked, but a couple are stamped with the insignia of the English army, like those they airdrop."

"Strange," said Pugliese.

"Strange," De Luca repeated. "In any case, somebody must have given them to him, he doesn't strike me as the kind of person who waits around for English airdrops."

"He sure doesn't," said Albertini, fixing a point midway between Pugliese and De Luca. "I went to PFR headquarters to get information, and, unbelievable, they were most kind. There was one fellow who was dying to talk, and he told me everything, though he wouldn't show me the file." He pulled a notebook out of his pocket and turned a page over. "Rehinard Vittorio," he read. "Born in Trento, on November 22, 1920. Member of the Fascist Republican Party since July 15, 1944. Membership passed thanks to the open sponsorship of Count Alberto Maria Tedesco. He had an assignment, was secretary of the office responsible for the Party's relationships with the Holy See and in particular with the Diocese, but nobody in there or at Party headquarters ever saw him. He sure liked the ladies, or rather, the ladies liked him; they'd run after him, and according to that officer, Rehinard was a kept man, because every time he'd meet him outside work he was always well-dressed, and he had some grand cars. He was a regular at the Spiritists' Club . . . "

"Spiritists' Club?"

De Luca remembered the visiting card he had found in Rehinard's wallet: *Sibilla*.

Albertini nodded, checking his notebook. "That's what they they call it, it's a group of people that gathered regularly at Rehinard's home; he was a real fanatic for all that's mystic, occult. They hold séances, things like that. But, what's important, often there are people outside of Tedesco's immediate circle, at least according to that guy, like Signora Alfieri."

"Alfieri?" De Luca frowned. "The wife of the Professor? He's another member of the government."

"Right." Albertini was so engrossed that he turned to De Luca. "And member of the faction opposing Tedesco's."

"It's called a wing, Albertini," Pugliese said.

"Whatever. Anyway, there's nothing more on Rehinard, no disciplinary orders, no admonitions . . . "

"And before that? Before July 15?"

"Before nothing, he wasn't a member of the PFR, he wasn't anywhere. Officially, Vittorio Rehinard's existence began four months ago."

De Luca sighed and shrugged his shoulders. He took the parcel of morphine from Pugliese and put it in his pocket.

"I don't believe any of this is much help," he said as if talking to himself. "A drug dealer that looks like the Count's personal middleman. And another member of the government like the Professor, Farinacci's friend. I see those passports getting nearer and nearer. Any sign of the porter?"

Albertini shook his head. "Ingangaro is on that," he said. "He's got his own idea."

De Luca removed himself from the car. He went towards the building, the parcel of morphine weighing in his pocket, twisting his trench coat to the point that he removed it and handed it to Marcon. As he entered, a wave of nausea suddenly broke over him. He put his hand over his stomach and remembered that he hadn't eaten. The nausea worsened when he saw the porter's quarters and recalled the intolerable odor of cabbage and stale air. For a second he considered retreating but then steeled himself and opened the door.

"Signora," he said, waiting to breathe. "I'd like to ask you another couple of questions." But nobody was in.

"Signora Galimberti," he called again, moving closer to the curtain that hid the rest of the apartment. He was forced to breathe and stifled a groan as his stomach turned. He pulled aside the curtain and suddenly his nausea passed. Signora Galimberti was lying on the floor under her chair, twisted up like a dry leaf. Her cranium had been smashed in.

"Christ almighty," murmured Pugliese at his shoulder. De Luca entered the room and crouched down, reaching out, but hesitated, not knowing exactly what to touch, then straightened up.

"It's useless," he said. "She's dead. Someone's split her head open. Murdered right under your nose, with the entire mobile squad and a platoon of militiamen. Congratulations." Albertini didn't reply, standing stiff at the door, his face green.

"If you have to vomit, go outside," said De Luca, leaving with him and bumping into Marcon, who was just then on his way in. He walked to the stairs and sat on a step, leaning his elbows on his knees and his face in his hands. He remembered that he had to shave.

"Someone must have seen her, too," said Pugliese. "At this point finding the porter becomes vital."

"Sure." De Luca closed his eyes and all of a week's sleep poured thickly over his eyelids, making him think for a second that despite everything, despite two murders in a single day, both of them on his shoulders, he was about to fall asleep right there.

"We'll have to question these idiots from the GNR," he said. "But with all the luck we're having today, I'll cut my own throat if somebody saw something. I want that porter. And I want that maid." He breathed deeply, gathering his strength, and then with a painful and sudden movement, he tore himself from the step and stood up. "Stay here," he told Pugliese. "Do what has to be done. I'm off."

"Good decision, Commissario. Get yourself some sleep."

"I'm not going home." De Luca moved towards the door. "I'm going to have my palm read."

CHAPTER FOUR

I t didn't seem much like a witch's lair. Seemed more like a doctor's office, elegant and quite ordinary, neat and clean. The only thing that gave the room a hint, a mere hint, of atmosphere was a sepia print showing the signs of the zodiac. De Luca was sitting stiffly on a sofa, arms folded over his chest, staring at a colored-glass door. He had given his visiting card to a little brunette, who was quite ordinary too, and was waiting for her return. In that still silence, punctuated only by the pitter-patter of rain that had started to fall against the panes of a square window just above his head, sleep once again began to overwhelm him, making him waver. He leaned his head back against the cool, white wall and fully emptied his lungs of air. He felt dirty, dusty, in tatters, and he would have liked a bath, to fall asleep in the bathtub, to melt into the water and slip away down the drain. Instead, enveloped in an electric haze, sitting beneath the patter of raindrops on the glass, he was having to wait for an old Gypsy with hoops in her ears and a turbid look in her eyes. He yawned, painfully, and closed his eyes. As he was reopening them, his vision still blurred, the glass door opened and Sonia Tedesco came out.

"Well, just look at that," said De Luca, surprised. Sonia lifted her chin, looking at him. She was very pretty, dressed in a black beret angled over her blond hair, a gray mantle thrown over her shoulders and a dress that fell down past her knees.

"Are you here to arrest me?" she asked.

"Have you done something wrong?" said De Luca. She grinned, curling up her red lips.

"You already used that line. You are all so boring . . . " She came towards him swaying and De Luca's blood began to run faster. Sonia lifted her leg up and put her knee over his, cross-wise, then leaned over him, caressing his face with her little, cold hand, and looked at him indifferently from under her eyelids, her red mouth half-closed and motionless.

"I'm always doing something wrong," she said, then moved her knee forward and touched him, again, once more causing him to jump back involuntarily. She smiled, slightly flattening out her lips, and lifted herself off him.

"Ciao policeman," she said. After a few wavering steps on her high heels she stopped. "That morning," she said, whirling the mantle around her, "I saw that harridan, Littorio's mother, as I was leaving."

"What?" De Luca got up from the sofa. "What did you say?" But she had already left; he was about to run after her when the little brunette called him from the glass door.

"The signora can see you now. If you wish to come this way . . . "

The witch had neither hoops in her ears nor a turbid look in her eyes. She wasn't even old. She was wearing a black turtleneck sweater and had an odd face with high cheekbones and eyes that were ever so slightly slanted, of a vague color, green, maybe brown; unusual, but nothing more. Her red hair fell over her forehead in long, wavy curls. Hard to say if she was beautiful. De Luca thought about it while entering a living room that was as anonymous and elegant as the waiting room. She watched him attentively, her elbows on a table, one hand cupped inside the other and her chin resting on them.

"I expected something more . . . mysterious," De Luca said. "Stuffed owls, black drapes . . . "

"This is my home," she responded. "I never work here. I go to my clients' homes." She had a low, rather deep voice that went up a pitch or two every so often as she opened up her vowels a little to accommodate a slight accent. She was probably from around Venice, or perhaps further northeast.

"Are you Comandante De Luca?"

"Commissario, I'm commissario now. That's an old card. And are you . . . Sibilla?"

"Valeria Suvich is my name. What are you here for?"

Valeria . . . De Luca smiled. "You should know, you're a clairvoyant, aren't you?"

But Valeria didn't smile. She pointed to a chair on the other side of the small, square table and brushed her hair from her forehead, staring at him as he sat down. She made him feel uneasy.

"As I told you, I never work at home," she said. "Only outside of here."

"And what is it you do?"

"I read the future. In the palms of people's hands, in the stars, in the cards, in coffee grounds . . . "

"And what do you see?"

"Whatever people want me to see."

"So, you're a charlatan."

"No. Do you want something to drink?"

De Luca nodded. The brunette had gone in a hurry, without saying goodbye, as in a few minutes the curfew would begin. She had left a round coffee table set with a bottle and two glasses that Valeria, turning in her chair, brought nearer with a dangerous clinking. She poured something resembling port into a glass and handed it to De Luca, and then poured another for herself. De Luca drank a sip, clenching his teeth as his empty stomach began to burn at once; instinctively he looked at Valeria as she drank and at the little ring of lipstick she left on the rim of the glass. It was light, too light.

"What do you want to know about Vittorio?" she asked after a moment of silence.

"You see, you are a clairvoyant," said De Luca. But again, no smile. "All that you're aware of. Did you know him well?"

"I'd see him every Friday at Tedesco's home. The Spiritists' Club. We read the cards, conducted séances . . . Vittorio was skeptical, he was always fooling around and the Count would get angry. Naturally, I was the medium."

"Who came to these Friday get-togethers?" De Luca finished his port and Valeria leaned forward to pour him another.

"Many people. Some came and went, others were regulars, like the Count and his daughter, Sonia. Then, there was Vittorio."

"And Signora Alfieri?"

"Yes, Silvia too. Her husband came occasionally, though when he was there, the Count wasn't. But Vittorio was always there, and often they'd speak at length, either before or after."

"Did you take drugs? You can tell me, if you want, I'm not interested in these things."

"No. Those tricks are too expensive for me. All I do is read people's eyes. Only Sonia would drink a lot; she was always drunk."

De Luca drank another sip, absentmindedly, and emptied the glass. A wave of heat rose to his face, making him flush, as the alcohol went faintly to his head and loosened his tongue. The first words came out a bit clumsily, but he managed to keep them under control.

"As far as you are aware, did Rehinard have a female companion?"

Valeria smiled, but it was a strange smile that moved only her bottom lip; more like she was wincing nastily rather than really smiling.

"Oh, he had many female companions. There isn't a well-born woman that hadn't been with Vittorio. He was very handsome, charming, and so delectably vain . . . Women found him attractive."

"Including you?"

Valeria's smile melted instantly and her lips closed. "Perhaps. Who knows? But I don't think that concerns you." She poured some more port into De Luca's glass but he stopped her, lifting the bottle up with two fingers.

"What is this, a magic potion?" he said. "Or are you trying to get me drunk? You've almost succeeded and I still have lots of questions to ask."

"Why are you so interested in this story?"

"It isn't that I'm interested, it's my job. I'm a policeman. I'd like to be a clairvoyant, like you, and see into the future to know how it'll end."

"I know how to read in the eyes, I told you."

"Really. And what do you see in mine?"

Valeria placed her chin in her hands again and looked him in the eyes, with a gaze so intense it ruffled him. He lowered his eyes and she, finally, smiled, this time for real.

"Fear," she said.

"Fear?" De Luca suppressed a shudder. "And what of? Let's skip this nonsense . . . Instead, tell me: what did the Count's daughter want? If I may ask, that is."

"You may not, but I will tell you anyhow. I'm like an aunt to her. She tells me all her problems and her affairs. She's having some trouble with her boyfriend, Alberto De Stefani."

De Luca groaned, annoyed. "Why, of course, the son of our Interior Undersecretary. What a mess this whole story is, I don't know which way to turn."

Valeria smiled again, lifting an eyebrow with an ironic look on her face, so ironic that De Luca felt he was being made fun of. He thought about it—to think about such a thing was odd—and decided she was beautiful, looking into her eyes lit up by that strange smile, and their color that changed when she moved into the light of the small lamp, turning red, magnetic, red like her hair.

"Are you trying to hypnotize me?" said De Luca, but just then a piercing cry of anguish wrenched him into a state of alert, paralyzing him for several seconds with his mouth and eyes wide open before he recognized the continuous and mechanical cry as the wail of a siren, outside, on the street. Valeria, too, had lost her allure completely and had stood up, knocking over a glass.

"My God!" she whispered. "The alarm. There's a bombing!"

She looked so terrified De Luca reached out and held her by the arm.

"Calm down," he said. "Let's go to the shelter. In the cellar, is it? Where is it?"

She didn't reply, completely petrified, eyes open staring at the window, her mouth trembling. The air around them began to vibrate, first outside, distant, then the windowpanes, the walls; a muffled drone getting stronger and closer, becoming a continuous, thick, heavy, ominous roar. Valeria hid her face in her hands, so De Luca took her in his arms, holding her tight, moving his fingers through her hair, on her neck, letting her stifle a cry against his shoulder. The roar became more intense, so near, everything was vibrating, windows, beams, furniture, Valeria was shaking and hanging on to him, digging her nails through his trench coat into his back. They heard a few isolated blasts from the antiaircraft fire, only a few, as ridiculous as hiccups amidst that mounting thunder. Then, just as it had arrived, the noise passed away, slowly, fading more and more, a distant drone, farther and farther away, and then, nothing. Also Valeria stopped shaking, little by little, with her face still pressed against De Luca's shoulder, warmed by his heavy, rapid breaths.

"They've gone," he said softly. "They were heading somewhere else, maybe Germany."

She didn't move.

"Forgive me," she murmured.

"You see," said De Luca, "you're frightened too. Just like me."

Valeria lifted her face and looked at him, dry-eyed, with those flecks of red, and her face very close to his, her lips parted and still trembling slightly. She tilted her head, closing her eyes, and kissed him, first softly, brushing against his mouth with her warm lips, then almost violently, pushing her lips against his, caressing his face, temples, head with her slender, soft hands, as he held her tight. She pushed him backwards, without letting him go, and he found himself on the sofa, clumsily twisted up in his trench coat, with her on top, kissing and caressing him. Valeria lifted herself up, looking at him with those strange, slanted eyes of hers, and crossed her arms in front of her, reached behind, and took off her sweater, beautiful, uncovering her breasts, her white shoulders and her neck, her red curls falling down over her forehead. She leaned forward, pushing against him, and he felt her skin, on fire, he breathed in her smell, strong and sweet, and lost himself in it, completely hypnotized, swept away, melting in a warm vortex that was burning everything, fear and exhaustion, anxiety and pain, more and more intense, faster and faster, to the end.

He awoke suddenly, without knowing where he was, as used to happen to him as a child, when he felt like he was upside down in the bed and no longer knew where his bedside table was, where the lamp was, lost in the night's darkness. But he was still on the sofa, stretched out on his stomach. Valeria was sitting next to him, leaning on her elbow, her head in her hand, looking down at him. She was wearing a nightgown, held closed with a safety pin, her hair pulled up and tied behind her head. She was beautiful. De Luca closed his eyes.

"What a strange thing," he said.

"What's so strange about it? We're both grown-ups."

"No, I didn't mean that. I meant . . . Well, I don't know what I wanted to say." He turned over and pulled himself back over the sofa, leaning his head in her lap. He felt her warmth again, and that sweet smell.

"I must have fallen asleep," he said. She nodded, smiling.

"You slept like a stone, like someone who hasn't slept in years. I even got up a couple of times, but you didn't notice. But you didn't sleep peacefully. You were talking."

"Oh, really? And what did I say?"

"Something ending in *red*."

"*Red*? Strange. Maybe I was dreaming about work."

Valeria stroked his forehead, brushing back his ruffled hair. She leaned forward and kissed him on the lips. Quickly.

"I know what kind of person you are."

"Do you? What kind of person am I?"

"One who hides."

"Who hides?"

"You're the kind that's always thinking about work, you even dream about it at night, the kind who's always busy, always on the run, never stopping."

"And this is what you call hiding?"

"Of course. In the middle of all this confusion, few people really know who they are and what they're doing, and this is why you hold on to your role, you who have got one, mentioning it whenever possible: I'm a policeman, I'm a policeman. That way you don't have to think about the front that's getting closer every day or about food rations. It's something I do too."

"Interesting. And so?"

"You are alone, but that doesn't worry you so long as work keeps you from thinking. In this, too, we're quite alike."

"Well, and how did you discover all this?"

"Your eyes. I know how to read the eyes. I read yours and I know you're frightened."

"You told me already. And what is it I'm afraid of?"

"That they'll kill you."

De Luca smiled, but his smile trembled a moment before opening completely and Valeria noticed. She kissed him again, and then lifted his head up.

"I'm going to make some coffee, real coffee," she said, standing.

De Luca put his hands behind his head and closed his eyes. He had almost fallen back asleep by the time she came back but the smell of coffee roused him. He sat up and took the cup from her, stirring the coffee with the teaspoon. He took a sip, scalding his lips.

"There's no sugar," he said, twisting his face up. Valeria sat down beside him, crossing her legs, and her nightgown fell open, revealing a round knee.

"All out," she said. "I put the teaspoon in just for decoration."

De Luca smiled and caressed her face, running his fingers through her hair. She leaned her head against his hand, nestling it against his shoulder, and just gazed at him slantwise.

"You really are a witch," he said.

"More than you think," she said. De Luca was about to lean forward, towards her lips, when a sudden thought crossed his mind, making him start. Without meaning to he brusquely pulled back his hand.

"The flashes," he said. "Good God, the flashes are *red*!"

He finished the coffee in a single go and stood up, pulling his clothes on as Valeria watched in surprise.

"Maybe you're right," he said, kissing her bare knee before leaving. "I really do dream about work while I'm asleep."

CHAPTER FIVE

He reached the station very early, so early the walls of the building across the street were still plastered with underground posters not yet discovered by the GNR patrols. For some time he and the guards were the only ones in the building, and in the dusty silence of the deserted bureau De Luca was uneasy, he felt he had to do something. He read the coroner's report that was lying on his desk, skimming over technical details, and stopping at the hypothesis that the suspect was *not a tall person, but nonetheless physically strong; standing in front of the victim, slightly to his left.* Everyone he had met until then had been "not tall." Sonia Tedesco, to name one. A turbid story of sex and drugs . . . She'd been in Rehinard's apartment that morning, this much was certain, she was drinking, then, zap! zap! Two stabs. Or the diminutive brunette in glasses, who knows, perhaps she was a jealous lover: she saw Sonia leaving, there was been an argument, and . . . Or . . . De Luca shook his head, too many gaps, too few elements to form any kind of theory. The maid was missing: she had to know a good many things, even if she had been away the three days before. And then the porter was missing: he knew something for sure, that is if, like his wife, he hadn't already been killed. And that damned paper knife was missing. And the SS. God almighty. De Luca shifted in his seat, its wood screeched impatiently, and looked at the clock. Outside in the corridor steps reverberated and now and then a door slammed. The station was coming back to life.

Pugliese was the first to arrive. He was wearing a light-colored summer coat, a flower in the buttonhole and a rather elegant pair of two-tone shoes. But with that hat and, above all, with that thin, angular face, he still looked like a cop. He had a newspaper under his arm and greeted De Luca with enthusiasm.

"Hey, Commissa! So, you're an early riser. Have you seen the papers? We're famous . . . You've shifted Socialization to page two."

He unfolded the paper, handing it to De Luca, who snatched it from him. On the front page there was an overblown three-column headline, *Mystery in via Battisti*, and underneath, a lead article full of bloody details. There was a picture of Vittorio Rehinard, who was described as a *scheming Freemason, a degenerate dedicated to vice and occult practices*. There were a few allusions to Count Tedesco, rather overt, principally to his daughter, whose relationship with Rehinard was *receiving close scrutiny from our vigilant police force's watchful eye*. The article also said that the case was in the hands of Commissario De Luca, *the Republic's most brilliant police investigator*.

"Absurd!" said De Luca. "Somebody has gone too far! All these macabre details, suspicions about eminent figures. They've violated all the Party directives on crime news!"

Pugliese smiled, pulling on his chin. "I have to admit that I haven't seen them come out with a *whodunit* like this since the days of the Girolimoni case. This is the final blow for us, ten to one they pull us off the case this morning and the censors'll confiscate the newspaper."

Albertini entered the office, he too with a newspaper under his arm.

"Have you seen?" he said waving the paper, then saw the copy lying on De Luca's desk and looked disappointed.

"We've seen it, all right," said Pugliese. "We'll be movie stars before long."

De Luca folded the newspaper and pushed it aside. All that attention bothered him, and scared him.

"Let's get back to serious matters," he said. "Far from brilliant investigator, I'm a fucking idiot. And you too, Pugliese."

"Me, Commissario?"

"The flashes, Pugliese, the flashes. That woman was talking about SS flashes, but they wear black flashes."

Pugliese frowned, bewildered. "I know, Commissario. I've seen quite a few."

"A few too many," said Albertini.

"Right!" De Luca slammed his fist down on the desk. "But the portress told us they were red! Red, get it!"

Pugliese hit his forehead and then gave himself a loud, theatrical slap across the face. "Jesus, that's right! Now I remember . . . red flashes. The Italian SS wear red flashes!"

"Exactly. It should be easy to find him now, the bastard; there aren't many Italian officers in the SS, and even fewer here in town. Albertini, this is a job for you. Go over to the headquarters of the Italian SS Legion, and find out what you can. Orders of De Luca, the most brilliant investigator in the Italian police."

Albertini didn't look too keen about it. He screwed up his face and looked over at Pugliese, who nodded. De Luca, who was in quite a state, didn't notice anything.

"We've got some news for you too," said Pugliese, taking off his coat and delicately hanging it on the hook on the back of the door. "Ingangaro did the rounds of the building and the maid's name has turned up: Assuntina Manna."

"Ah, finally! And where is she?"

Pugliese shrugged. "Eh, Commissa, they call them evacuees precisely because they don't have homes and it's not easy to find them. But right now Ingangaro is over at Social Security and the labor department and sooner or later he'll find her, you'll see."

Two knocks on the door made them turn. A guard, beret in hand, appeared at the door.

"Commissario?" he said. "The Chief wishes to see you. Immediately."

De Luca opened his arms wide and shook his head.

"See?" he said. "Say goodbye to our case. Pity, though, I was growing fond of it."

Dressed in a tailored pinstripe suit, the Chief was waiting for him at the door to his office, wearing a smile that revealed a gold tooth.

"Commissario!" he said cordially, taking De Luca by the arm and accompanying him to a seat in front of his desk. Vitali was in the office too, in uniform, sitting in an armchair, one leg still dangling over the armrest. It looked as if he hadn't moved since their last meeting. The Chief sat down at his desk, slipped on a pair of heavy-rimmed glasses and began thumbing through the typewritten reports that were sitting before him upon an open newspaper, murmuring "good, good." De Luca was still standing, quite surprised by this unexpected greeting.

"As you will have noticed," said Vitali, twirling the eagle-crested beret around his finger, "you have total support and collaboration from the entire national press. Only someone who fears fascist justice, someone who, hiding in the shadows, is preparing to betray, may attempt to hinder your progress. But the police must cry the firmest 'I-don't-care-a-damn,'" and he really did cry it, "in the face of those who exert political pressure of any kind on the working of justice. Am I right, Chief?"

"Absolutely right," burst out the Chief. "Do have a seat, De Luca, and bring us up to date. Your reports are clearly pointing in a direction, it seems . . . "

"More than one direction," said De Luca, and began telling them what had been going through his head minutes before in his office. But when he got to Sonia Tedesco, the Chief interrupted him, pointing his glasses at him.

"There!" he said. "That's the right idea. The Count's daughter is a sort of madwoman, a reckless youth flitting from one bed to another throughout the entire city and has embarrassed her father on more than one occasion."

"Who certainly doesn't need her help to make a fool of himself," said Vitali and the Chief laughed.

"Isn't it practically obvious, De Luca," he said. "That she's the person we're looking for?"

De Luca nodded, thoughtfully, searching for the best words to say what he wanted in the right way. A wary disquiet, verging on fear, made him shift uncomfortably in his seat.

"Many of our leads seem to point in her direction, that's true," he said. "But there are further elements that must be taken into account. There's all that morphine we found in Rehinard's house. From whom did he get it? Who did he give it to? Not all to Sonia Tedesco . . . And Rehinard's relationship with the Spiritists' Club isn't clear—"

"Degenerates, scoundrels, and Freemasons," said Vitali. The Chief nodded seriously.

"Many people were part of the Club," De Luca continued. "Signora Alfieri, for example."

The Chief dropped his glasses as Vitali stood. "Silvia Alfieri?" they said in unison, then Vitali gestured to the Chief to ensure that he would get the next word.

"I categorically exclude it!" he said. "Absolutely not! Professor Alfieri is a distinguished gentleman, a lifelong fascist, and a member of the government. What's more . . . Silvia! A woman who has given her country one son fallen at the Russian front and another serving in the SS!"

De Luca started, making his chair squeak.

"What did you say?" he asked. Vitali smiled, pleased by the effect he had had.

"Young Littorio," he said. "An example of how the Alfieri family battles for the ideals of the Italian Social Republic! Forget it, De Luca, this is . . . what do you investigators call it? A false lead. Just follow the Tedesco lead, go straight as an arrow . . . Did you know he called yesterday afternoon to have you pulled off the case? Doesn't that already seem like a confession . . . ? I am not a policeman, but I sense certain things." He touched his nose, sniffing the air a couple of times. "I sense them! There's the smell of wild jealousy, orgies, Masonic rites . . . This is the right direction!"

"The right direction!" echoed the Chief.

De Luca watched them stiffly, his skin crawled and he nodded slowly.

"Will do," he said. "Will do."

Pugliese was putting all the copies of the report into a blue folder with Ingangaro's help. He also put a copy of the newspaper in.

"Here you are," he said when De Luca came in. "If you'll just tell me who I have to hand it over to . . . "

"We're not handing over anything," said De Luca. "On the contrary!" He looked at Ingangaro, reflecting. "Do me a favor," he said. "I haven't had breakfast. Go get me a cappuccino . . . anything. Whatever you want."

He put some money in his hand and pushed him out, then turned to Pugliese, who was looking at him, lips protruding in a worried look.

"What's happened, Commissa?"

"We're in deep shit," said De Luca. He fell heavily into the chair behind his desk, joined his hands in front of his face and closed his eyes. "We're being used. We're right in the middle of a political struggle between the Professor's and Tedesco's cliques. Vitali is using us as a personal weapon to damn well disgrace Tedesco. They don't give a damn about the murder." Pugliese whistled, slowly. "Fucking hell," he murmured. "I've never liked these kinds of things. Back then, I refused to go into the Fascist Secret Service precisely because I wanted to avoid certain kinds of trouble."

"I don't like them either." De Luca opened his eyes. "We're like soldiers at war in this story, Pugliese, and you know what happens to soldiers if they're not careful? They get killed."

Pugliese lowered his eyes, passing his hand over his greased-down hair. That slow, stiff movement made him look just like a raven.

"Let's have some men follow Tedesco," he said decisively, in a tone that seemed more like an order than a suggestion. "Let's have Sonia tailed by men I know, men who'll report back. You wanted to interrogate the Count? Bring him in, even escorted, let's do what they want. Right now, just when Ingangaro had discovered where the porter—"

De Luca raised his head suddenly.

"Galimberti? And where is he?"

"Nearby and far away at the same time. In this very street, number 21."

"So? What's at number 21?"

"The Gestapo, Commissario. They arrested him yesterday."

De Luca bit his lip, cupping his chin with his hand. He sighed, thinking of the Gestapo, the Chief, the Federale . . . Stick to Tedesco, stick to Tedesco . . .

"Let's go," he said, standing. "Put whoever you want on the Count. In the meantime, we'll move ahead alone."

*

At the Gestapo they had to wait in the corridor, seated on an appallingly uncomfortable strip wooden window-seat. From the office next to them came the incessant clatter of a typewriter, rapid-fire like a machine gun; the building was alive with movement, with soldiers coming and going. Pugliese seemed nervous, sitting straight, hat in hand, and every so often he slid a finger under his collar, behind his black policeman's tie. After ten minutes or so the clatter suddenly stopped. The office door opened and a corporal motioned them in, closing the door behind them. He returned to the typewriter, hands joined over the keys, while a lieutenant in a black uniform, armband and silver flashes, leaned against a table holding one of De Luca's cards in his hand. He studied them with his blue eyes for a few seconds before speaking.

"Would you show me your papers please?"

He said *vould*, like in those American movies from before the war. De Luca handed him his badge. Another moment of silence.

"So you are the famous Commissario De Luca," said the lieutenant. "My name is Dietrich. What a pleasure to meet you." Just like in the movies, *vhat*.

"The pleasure is mine."

De Luca hesitated, disturbed by the lieutenant's cold, limp, flabby blue stare fixed silently on him. Motionless, the corporal looked at him in the same way.

"And?" said the lieutenant and De Luca roused himself.

"We believe you've arrested a man," he said firmly. One had to appear determined with the Germans, this much he knew. "Just yesterday. Oreste Galimberti. This man is crucial for an investigation being conducted by the Republican Police and we'd like to interrogate him. Only to ask him a few questions." De Luca had considered asking them to hand

Galimberti over, but then convinced himself it was an absurd request.

"A police investigation?" asked the lieutenant.

"Yes. A murder."

"But you have documents of the Brigata Ettore Muti, special division of the Political Police, *nicht wahr*?"

De Luca sighed. "Yes, that's true, but now I'm with the Police. If you require authorization or want me to call the Chief, I'll do so at once." He was bluffing, but it didn't show. The lieutenant just looked at him, in silence, leaning against the table with his lanky legs stuck into black boots. De Luca felt that he was about to lose his patience, a dangerous sensation that sent a chill through him. Beside him, Pugliese shifted slightly, imperceptibly, brushing against his arm.

"That won't be necessary," said the lieutenant all of a sudden. "I am pleased to assist you. Before the war I too was in the *Kriminalpolizei*."

He said something to the corporal, who jumped up and brought over a black bound register. The lieutenant took it from him and began thumbing through some pages.

"What was it you said? Galimberti, with a G, like gate. Galimberti, Galimberti, Galimberti, Oreste. Yes. Arrested on April 17, 1945 at 11 A.M. after an anonymous complaint of suspected terrorist activities. Yes, he's here."

De Luca, with beating heart, held his breath. "Can I see him?"

"Yes, you can. Ah, one moment. I see that his name is *vernichtet*. Discharged. He is no longer here at the Gestapo."

De Luca's fists tightened, another second and he would start shouting.

"Who has him now?" he hissed. "Have you given him to the Brigata Muti? To the Decima Mas? You can tell me, I—"

"That is confidential," said the lieutenant, tracing the register's entry with his finger. "But I can bend the rules for a . . .

what is it you say? A *colleague*. And what a coincidence!" A smile escaped his lips. "He's passing by right this minute."

He pointed over their shoulders to a window that opened onto a courtyard; De Luca turned and hurried to look out, followed by Pugliese.

"*Ein Unfall*," said the lieutenant. "An accident . . . It happens, sometimes."

In the courtyard, two SS wearing leather aprons were loading the bloodied corpse of an old man onto a truck.

"Now what?"

Pugliese was in the driver's seat, his hands draped over the steering wheel. Beside him, De Luca wore a dark look and kept his chin buried in his trench coat.

"Now what?" he said, irritated. "Is that all you can say?"

"No, but I'm asking you, you're the boss," Pugliese replied, offended. "I know what has to be done. Arrest Sonia Tedesco and we're through with it."

De Luca turned to face him. He sighed and buried himself back in his trench coat.

"Too easy," he said.

"And we don't like the easy way, do we?"

"No, we don't. If only Galimberti hadn't gotten himself nabbed like that . . . Because I don't believe that phone call accusing him just now is a mere coincidence; there are sixteen different police forces in the Republic and all of them are arresting someone, but I don't believe it just the same. He could have told us a lot of things, like which of those women was the last up in Rehinard's apartment that morning, because as far as I see it, a woman did it. Rehinard must have had dozens of enemies, but not the kind who go around killing like that, as if by chance, with a paper knife found on a desk. They'd make him disappear, like Galimberti, or they'd shoot him in the street. And sex has something to do with it, because of that second wound . . . Sonia Tedesco, or the Professor's wife, whom everyone is trying to protect. Or maybe someone else we know nothing about." He thought about Valeria, for a split second, but long enough to make him shake his head as if shooing away a bothersome mosquito. Not Valeria. Why not?

"Too many missing pieces," he said loudly, though speaking to himself.

"We need more information on Alfieri's wife," Pugliese said. "But given the situation, we're never going to have any. If we go asking questions about them everyone from the Chief to Il Duce himself will know about it in no time, and then, say goodbye!"

De Luca bit his lip nervously. He was refusing to think about it, but an idea had surfaced a few minutes before, and it persisted, badgering him more by the minute. The effort needed to put aside his suspicions about Valeria without betraying his policeman's nature had cleared his mind.

"I'll take care of that," he said darkly. "I know where to find the information we need."

CHAPTER SIX

I t was an old farmhouse with charred, crumbling walls, without any more roughcast, almost in the countryside, in an area the city had reached before the war transforming it into a suburb. So black, solid, and squat was the building, it almost looked like a convent, isolated from the other houses, on the edge of a potholed road with no sidewalk. On the wall, low, far from the door, there was a message painted in red smudged letters: *Get ready, murderers.*

De Luca made the car pull up at the corner, at a distance, so that the guard, looking at them from the door, machine gun slung over his shoulder, wouldn't come down. He got out and signaled Pugliese to go. He crossed the dusty road with a purposeful stride, hands out of his pockets, far from his body, and as he got nearer to the ravaged façade, to the half-open front door, to the crumbling steps, the place's familiarity assuaged that heavy anxiety oppressing him. A vague sense of unease, hidden somewhere between his stomach and his heart, was all that was left.

"Good morning, Comandante," said the guard, recognizing him, greeting him with a stiff-arm salute. De Luca didn't respond, didn't even look at him, and walked straight in through the main door as the guard turned to observe him, unsure whether he should stop him or not.

And inside, too, nothing had changed. There was hardly any light, even with the windows open, and a persistent odor, a mixture of alcohol and dust. Closed doors of old wood with new locks. An inept typist's infrequent chatter, a two-fingered tap, tap, tap. De Luca climbed the stairs, brushing lightly against the handrail, nodded to someone he passed by, and stopped in front of an office, its door as impersonal as all the others. Far away, downstairs, echoed something that seemed like a scream. De Luca knocked at the door.

"Come in," said a voice bearing a hint of a Sardinian accent. De Luca entered without hesitation, decisively, as he had a hundred times before.

"It's me," he said.

Seated behind his desk, Captain Rassetto, hand mid-air holding a pen, looked at him surprised. He was a thin man, with black, curly hair combed back, and a short, fine mustache flush with his lip. He had pitch-black eyes that were close together, giving his face a sharp look, like that of a falcon.

"Of all things," he said, and his Adam's apple moved up and down his slender neck, between pointed chin and the uniform's collar. "I was convinced I wouldn't see you again." From under the desk he pushed forward, with a booted foot, a chair that De Luca caught by the back before it fell. Rassetto looked at him, smiling, uncovering sharp teeth, wolf-like.

"I hear things are going well for you," he said. "You've become famous. Who knows, maybe they'll promote you, maybe they'll make you Chief in place of that guy. What is it: feeling nostalgic for your old office?"

"I'm quite happy at the police," said De Luca, "It's interesting work." He wanted to say "clean," but didn't.

Rassetto nodded. He knocked the pen against his brilliant white teeth, then stood up and walked over to the window, thumbs hooked over his belt. "You know, they threw a couple of bombs into the courtyard," he said, as if distracted. "They get bolder and more arrogant by the day. They killed

Foschini the other day, right out front. You remember Foschini, right?"

De Luca remained silent. Rassetto walked back to his desk and shuffled through the papers scattered on top. He picked up a yellow one and sent it scudding through the air toward De Luca, who caught it on the fly as it was planing lightly along the floor.

"Might interest you," said Rassetto, turning back to the window. De Luca began reading. It was a statement from the CLN, the National Liberation Committee, containing a list of names that began with Rassetto's. In the fifth place was his own.

"Surprised?" Rassetto asked without turning. "You thought you were out of it only because over here you did brain work? Or because you got yourself transferred?"

"Well, yes, I am surprised. I'm a policeman," said De Luca.

Rassetto turned, wearing his triangular smile.

"And we aren't?" he said, leaning his hands on the desktop. "Listen De Luca, you've always been clever, and you did good work; that's why I backed your request when you decided to return to the police. But don't kid yourself, don't think that you've got your virginity back because now you're chasing chicken thieves. You've seen the CLN's directives on what to do with the 'murderers' from the Brigate Nere."

"But I'm with the police."

"Oh come on, how can you be so naive? If things end badly, if the *banditen* take over the streets, we'll all be up against a wall within an hour, me in the middle, you on one side, and Valente, the dentist, on the other; like Jesus and the two thieves. But I don't care a damn." He straightened up, hanging his thumbs back on his belt. "Because we're going to win. What is it you want from me? You want to make your way up the party ladder? You want a good conduct badge saying you've been a longstanding member of the fascist ranks?"

De Luca roused and, with effort, concentrated on the case. He dropped the yellow leaflet onto the pile of papers and forced himself not to look at it.

"I need a favor," he said. "I'm in deep shit. I want information on Alfieri, I know there's a dossier in the files."

Rassetto stared into space for a while. He seemed preoccupied, but De Luca knew he was thinking, and when he behaved that way, with that strange half smile, something dangerous was always on the way.

"Fine," he said. "I'll give you the information. Hell, Alfieri rubs me the wrong way, too. But in return I want you to tell me the whole story and to keep me updated on everything that concerns him."

De Luca nodded.

"Listen, then. Fabio Alfieri is an ironclad fascist, a friend of Farinacci and of the Germans. He's an anti-Semite of the Preziosi School, one of the most intransigent. But he's playing it both ways. He's in contact with the CLN on behalf of the Germans, through the Curia; he's conveniently keeping a number of doors open. Every now and again he smuggles out a Jew, or an important Red, getting ready for what'll come, the bastard. His son, Littorio, a model fascist, and officer in the SS, acts as the go-between. Twice a month he goes to Verona in civvies. His wife, on the other hand, spends every Friday at Tedesco's house, Alfieri's sworn adversary, who's more conservative than fascist, another double-crosser, but with the English. They're all getting ready to give up shamefully, these fine gentlemen, and they're competing with one another to do it in the safest way possible. It's disgusting." Rassetto scowled gnashing his teeth, then went back to the dangerous smile. "Anyway, Signora Alfieri has been spending quite a lot of nights out lately, I had her followed. In Via Battisti, I don't remember the number. The Alfieris are a hell of a family, eh? Now it's your turn."

De Luca told him everything, speaking mainly to himself; about Sonia and the pressure from Vitali, the porter, the morphine, and the missing maid. He left out only Valeria. He had spoken so quickly that when he finished he was breathing heavily, under Rassetto's amused look.

"Quite a fucking mess," he said. "Good luck."

"Thanks."

"Don't mention it. And remember: whenever you want to come back here, you're always welcome."

"Thanks," De Luca repeated, getting to his feet.

He walked out of the office with the memory of that fluttering yellow sheet of paper, planing lightly through the air, forcibly ignored, amid his thoughts. From downstairs echoed another indistinct, far-off scream.

It was fast getting dark when he got back to town and the curfew was about to come into force. He hadn't called Pugliese to come and pick him up, preferring to walk alone, grim and silent, hands in his pockets, through the streets that were growing darker and more deserted, past streetlamps turned off for blackout. It was warm, summer was finally on its way, and a balmy wind, its squalls full of dust, plastered the flaps of his trench coat against his legs.

De Luca was thinking things over, completely absorbed by a horde of thoughts knocking against one another, getting in each other's way, eluding his attempts to put them in order. The yellow sheet of paper, Sonia, Silvia, Valeria . . . He'd called Valeria twice that day without ever getting hold of her, and decided to go there, even though he had phoned ten minutes earlier. Perhaps he would wait for her in front of the house, but he really needed to see her, even if only to talk, or to be seen by those oblique witch's eyes flecked with red. He picked up his pace, passively falling into the rhythm of his own steps. A man bent over a bicycle passed him pedaling fast. Up ahead of him the tail of a patrol turned a corner without noticing him. De Luca reached inside his trench coat to get his badge just in case someone stopped him, but as he was pulling it out of his pocket it slipped from his hand. Kneeling down to pick it up with an annoyed sigh, he noticed a man behind him in a short coat who stopped abruptly to tie his shoe in front of a closed shop window. His heart started beating a bit faster. De Luca turned and started walking again, stiffly. Further ahead, on the left, a sudden movement disappeared around the corner. He grew tense, slipped a hand into his pocket and placed it on his gun. The effort not to turn around made his neck muscles hurt as he quickened the pace, ears alert to the sound of steps behind him. When he saw the man on the bicycle standing at the end of the street, checking the chain, he hadn't the slightest doubt. An icy chill ran up his spine, making him shake beneath his trench coat. He turned right suddenly down the first street he came across, and started running as fast as he could. He heard a whistle behind him and a sound of rapid footsteps following him as he turned right again and then left, with no idea where he was heading. He came out into a small square, and thought the game was up, as near to him there was only a long row of buildings, front doors closed, and ahead a street without cover. He looked around, panting, the footsteps getting closer, and recognized something familiar, a terrace towering above him, Valeria's apartment. He pushed the front door, which opened and hit the wall with a thud, then ran up the stairs clutching the handrail. He reached Valeria's door and starting beating against it desperately with his closed fist.

"Dear God," he said aloud. "Please let her be home!"

He stopped knocking and listened, mouth open, holding his breath. There was a sound of footsteps, of shoes scuffling, from the stairs, so he pulled out his pistol and continued pounding on the door with his other hand.

"Coming. I'm coming!" said a voice from behind the door, almost drowned out by the banging. "Who *is* it?"

De Luca stopped knocking, he slid the pistol's bolt and the footsteps stopped, leaving behind a wary silence.

"Open the door!" he cried. "It's me. Open the door."

Valeria opened the door, and De Luca threw himself in, pushing her to one side.

"Close it!" he wheezed, panting. She opened her mouth, then saw the pistol and started. She closed the door at once, putting the chain on. De Luca took her by the arm and pulled her away, past the glass door, into the living room. He closed that door too, leaning a chair against it, while Valeria looked at him wide-eyed.

"What's happening?" she asked him. "What is it?"

"The phone," said De Luca. Valeria pointed at it, on a table near the window, and he lifted the receiver and dialed a number, without putting down the pistol. While he was waiting he cautiously looked out the window. In the street there was the man in the coat leaning against a wall.

"Pugliese? Thank God! I thought I'd never get you. I need help, three men are following me, they're out to kill me. Call somebody and come over right away!" He gave the address and hung up, glancing outside once more. The man in the coat was talking to the man dressed in the jacket, and both were looking up. Valeria came close, held his arm, and looked out too.

"Who are they?" she asked.

"Tedesco's men, I think. Or maybe Alfieri's."

"Perhaps they're partisans."

De Luca turned his head slightly, with a tense jerk, then looked back at once to the street below.

"No, I don't believe so. I don't know. I don't think so."

"Sit down. They're not going to come in through the window, are they?"

She pushed him onto the sofa and sat down next to him, folding her legs beneath her. She caressed his cheek with the back of her hand.

"You're shaking," she said. De Luca put away the pistol. He bit his lip nervously.

"I was scared," he said. "That was really close." She leaned forward, slipping an arm around his shoulders, bringing his head down to one side, maternally, but he was too tense and stood up at once, pacing the room.

"I want to ask you something," he said without looking at her. "Were you in Rehinard's apartment that morning?"

"Why are you asking?"

"Because I want to know. Did you go to his house that morning?"

Valeria sighed. "I was there, yes. But I didn't kill him."

"Why were you there?"

"Because I knew him. I often went there."

"Why?"

"What is this, an interrogation?"

"Yes, it is." De Luca looked at her, sitting upright on the sofa in a dressing gown, her eyes fixed on him, coldly. He couldn't bear her look and began walking up and down again.

"Were you sleeping with him?" he asked.

"That is none of your business."

"No. It is my business. Rehinard has been killed, and I'm a cop!"

Valeria sprung up and a lock of wavy red hair fell over her eyes. "If you want to take your fear out on somebody because you were scared," she hissed, "do it with someone else! Yes, I slept with him. He was very handsome and I'm an adult, and a free woman. I also slept with you, didn't I? Do I have to justify that as well?"

She turned her back to him. De Luca remained silent, his eyes downcast. He gazed at the dressing gown's hem, flowing against her exposed ankles, above the round heels left bare by her slippers.

"When you were there, did you enter his studio?" he asked calmly, in a level voice.

"Yes."

"What was on the table? The little one?"

Valeria remained with her back turned, silent, as if concentrating.

"There were two glasses," she said after what seemed an eternity. "One had lipstick on it. I even teased him about it a little. I wasn't jealous; he meant nothing to me."

Outside on the street a car stopped with a screech of brakes. De Luca ran to the window and saw Pugliese and Albertini getting out of the car and Marcon, machine gun in arm, standing on the running board.

"They're here," he said. "I'll head down. Don't be afraid, no one will come to bother you."

Valeria shrugged. He waited. He would have liked to hear her say, "Stay here," he would have liked to ask her, but she didn't say it and he didn't ask. He went down the stairs, where Pugliese was leaning against the wall waiting for him, pistol in hand.

They dropped him off at the door of the pension in which he lived and waited until he'd opened it, Marcon, machine gun still in his hands, standing on the running board keeping an eye on the street, and Pugliese leaning out of the car window with his pistol drawn. Only when he waved them away, insisting, did they leave.

Now that the fear had subsided, De Luca started thinking again and decided that it had been Tedesco's men. In the car he'd talked about it with Pugliese, and even he agreed that the Professor had nothing to gain from eliminating him, given that they were virtually working for him. But also Pugliese had thrown a question out to him, nearly mumbling, using more or less the same words as Valeria: "What if they were partisans?" De Luca hadn't answered.

He went up the stairs cast into darkness by the blackout, holding on to the handrail, and began fishing in his pocket for the key to his room. He was exhausted and thought that finally, the minute he reached the bed, he would fall into a heavy, leaden sleep. But when he arrived on the landing a strange sound, a sigh or a sob, made him press himself against the wall, his heart throbbing madly again. He made out a light-colored shape, crumpled up near his door, seated. Though it was dark he recognized it immediately, and stopped, hand in his pocket on the pistol's butt.

"Good God," murmured De Luca, getting his breath back. "You scared me."

Sonia Tedesco was sitting on the floor, arms around her knees, curled up beneath a white raincoat. She watched him wide-eyed and seemed to be trembling.

"What are you doing here?" De Luca asked, but she didn't reply. She was really trembling. De Luca opened the door with his key, then took her by the arm, pulled her to her feet. They entered the apartment, a bare-looking bedroom, containing a table, a chair, and a small armchair in the corner. Sonia sat down in the armchair and pulled her legs up, wrapping herself up in the raincoat and just looked at him, perched, eyes open like an owl.

"I've had too many thrills today," said De Luca. "And I'm not really in the mood for playing games."

"There's a man following me," said Sonia all of a sudden. De Luca smiled tiredly.

"Really?" he said sarcastically. "What a surprise!"

He took the chair by the backrest and brought it close to the armchair, sitting in front of Sonia, as for an interrogation. She backed up, curling up even more inside her raincoat. She was pale, with damp hair stuck to her forehead. There was something strange about her, De Luca noticed it a few minutes later: her eyes were wide and not half-closed as always, giving her a look that was less sensual but more infantile and frightened.

"It wasn't me," she said. De Luca spread open his arms.

"I'm starting to believe it."

"So why is there always someone following me? Someone is spying on us, on Alberto and me, friends are avoiding us . . . And then the newspapers . . . " She stirred in the armchair and put a hand in a pocket of her raincoat, quickly and clumsily, then in the other, pulling out something that fell from her hand and hit the floor with a heavy thud. She was about to bend forward to pick it up but De Luca was quicker and instinctively held her arm back, even before realizing that it was a small automatic.

"Good lord," he muttered. "This really is a bad habit." He pushed Sonia back in the armchair and picked up the pistol, holding it in his palm with only a slight, belated trace of fear, a quick shudder that vanished immediately. Perhaps it was true that he had had too much excitement that night.

"I'd like to drink something," said Sonia, avoiding looking at him.

"Me too, but there isn't anything. Wait, maybe I have something . . . "

He went over to a table and opened a draw, finding an almost empty bottle of Arzente. He poured it into a glass, took a sip, then brought it to Sonia and watched as she tossed it down. He smiled when he noticed the red mark the glass had left on her cheeks, just like on a child.

"It wasn't me," she repeated. De Luca sighed, turned the chair around, and straddled it, but he stood up immediately because it seemed too much like an interrogation. He sat on the bed, making the springs squeak.

"What an ugly mess," he said to Sonia's motionless profile, all curves, under the damp fringe. "Whatever I do is wrong. If I follow you, your father'll have me killed, if I don't, Vitali'll kill me. If I investigate, I'm dead. If I don't investigate, I'm dead the same. Is this any way to work?"

Sonia's profile remained silent, but De Luca wasn't looking for replies.

"I was born curious, that's my problem. It's always been the same . . . Everything has to be clear, everything in order, even the slightest detail, with a rational how and why, otherwise I go out of my mind. This is why I can't just arrest you and act like nothing happened, because I *know* that the investigation wouldn't be over. At the same time, I can't ignore you; I have to keep a tail on you because the rich and powerful are at each other's throats all around you and me, and a poor cop who's too curious can disappear quickly. I mean, really, is this any way to work?" He took the glass from her hand and throwing his head back drained the last drop. It seemed like she wasn't listening to him; precisely for this, De Luca continued speaking, as if to himself.

"When they called me into the Muti special division I went immediately, jumping at the chance. Because at the Muti you could do good work, get it?" She didn't get it, wasn't even listening. "There everything was so efficient, there were the best investigators, the best police records, there were resources . . . Police work has always been like this and it's what I've always done. You don't ask a policeman to make political choices, you ask him to do his job well. That's why I'm convinced those men before work for your father and are not partisans . . . "

But what about Rassetto's list? he asked himself silently, sneeringly, as if it were someone else asking.

Sonia moved, turning her face slowly towards him, looking at him again with half-open eyes, though her forehead still did seem covered in sweat.

"Do you want to make love to me?" she said all at once, somewhat absently, and he was startled, momentarily, for his thoughts had been altogether far from there. Even before he had a chance to reply, Sonia stood up and De Luca reached out, as she seemed about to fall. But she regained her balance, staggering, pulled her raincoat tight and looked around as if she didn't know where she was.

"He's hiding," she said. "But he's spying on me . . . He's spying on me." She took a step towards De Luca, then abruptly changed direction and quickly, though a bit unsteady on her heels, moved to the door.

"You can't go out," said De Luca. "There's the curfew . . . " But he mouthed it in a low voice, and she didn't seem to hear him. She went out, leaving him alone, sitting there on the bed, tired, exhausted and thoroughly convinced that he wouldn't be getting any sleep that night either.

CHAPTER SEVEN

"Our Ingangaro is a real mastiff, Commissario. When he says he'll find someone, he does, like that poor porter. Assuntina Manna is over there." Pugliese pointed to a wooded shack with a sheet-metal roof, the only one with a door and a real window, shut. Drying clothes were hanging from a cord that ran between the shack and what was left of a bombed wall, curved and cracked, that hung over it. There wasn't a soul around, not even a woman or a child playing, perhaps because of the car, or big Marcon's copper's mug waiting for them behind the drying clothes, big hands in his pockets and hat pulled down over his eyes.

De Luca got out of the car, followed by Pugliese, and walked towards the shack, detecting a certain feeling of being observed. He rapped twice sharply on the wooden door, as Pugliese worriedly looked up at the wall.

"Aren't these people afraid it'll come down on their heads?"

De Luca knocked again, harder. "Police, open up immediately!" he said. He was about to knock again when the door opened and a robust young man with curly hair, dressed in an old army sweater, came out on the threshold, blocking the entrance.

"Police," De Luca said. "We're looking for Assuntina Manna."

The man glowered at him, arms crossed over his large chest.

"She ain't here," he said harshly. "She isn't here no more."
He stepped back as if to leave, but Pugliese moved forward and
put his hand against the door, stopping him from closing it.

"I know this gentleman," he said. "Bruno Manna. You've
been our guest on a number of occasions, haven't you, young
man?" Marcon, too, had moved closer. He put his hand on
Bruno's arm, but he jerked it free.

"Get your hands off me," he snarled. "Assuntina ain't
here!" He tried to get back inside, but they were all too close.
He leaned a hand on De Luca's chest and shoved him back
and as De Luca clutched his arm to stop himself falling, he
kicked him between the legs. De Luca groaned and fell down
on one knee as Pugliese grabbed the man by his sweater, losing his hat. Marcon moved in and socked him hard in the
stomach, folding him in two, then grabbed him by the neck,
hitting him again while Pugliese tried to handcuff him. The
face of an old woman, frightened, appeared from behind the
door, then a young girl came out and started to scream and
tear out Marcon's hair.

"Bruno! Dear Lord, what are you doing to him? *Bruno!*"

"Run, Assuntina!" the man cried. "Leave her alone. She's
got nothing to do with it."

"Stay still, you bastard," yelled Marcon, trying to hold him.

"Holy *Christ!*" De Luca shouted. He sprang to his feet and
grabbed Assuntina by the arm, pulling her away as Pugliese
kicked Bruno, dropping him to his knees. He dragged her
around the corner of the house and pushed her back against
the wooden planks, holding her arm and shaking her, as she
wouldn't stop yelling.

"Stop it, for God's sake, stop it! I just want to ask you some
questions."

Assuntina finally stopped, so De Luca led her behind the
wall and sat her down on a rock. When she tried to kneel,
hands joined, he sat her back down again.

"Keep calm," he told her. "Nothing's going to happen to Bruno and nothing is going to happen to you, don't worry. I'm not here to arrest anybody. Holy cow, try to understand that."

Assuntina lowered her eyes and wrapped her arms around herself, smothering her sobs. She was a beautiful girl, very young, with dark skin and black eyes, wearing a light, red-checkered dress that had slipped off her round shoulder during the struggle.

"Listen, will you," said De Luca. "You were Vittorio Rehinard's maid, right?"

Assuntina, behind the black ruffled hair that had fallen over her face, nodded with a sigh that was sucked back in by a sob. De Luca put his foot up onto the rock and bent forward, as it was still hurting where he had been kicked. He put a finger under her chin, forcing her to lift her head and look at him.

"You got a tongue, kid, or do I have to take you to the station?"

"I was Signor Rehinard's servant," Assuntina whispered, then she cleared her throat and repeated the words. "I was Signor Rehinard's servant, but it's already been six days since he sent me away."

"You haven't been to his house since then?"

"No," she sobbed. "No, no."

"Why'd he send you packing?"

"I don't know. He's like that, after a while he got tired of his maids and he'd send them away. He'd told me that sooner or later he'd send me away too." She sobbed. Tears began falling down her full, childish cheeks. De Luca let her lower her chin and pulled himself from the rock. He was about to lean on the wall but stopped himself just in time.

"What did Signor Rehinard do?" he asked. "Did he stay at home? Did he go out? Did he see people?"

Assuntina dried her tears with her wrist and nodded, but the tears started falling again instantly. "He went out every morning, late, and Friday nights. A lot of people came by, but I didn't know anyone."

"Can you describe them?"

"There were always lots of ladies. And a soldier."

"What did they do with Signor Rehinard? Did they talk? Did they bring him anything?"

Assuntina shook her head and let out another sob. "I don't know," she said. "He would send me out on errands. Sometimes he would tell me to stay out the whole night."

"Was there a blond girl?"

"Yes, many times. One morning I found her outside on the steps, crying. Signor Rehinard let her in and when she came out, she was . . . I don't know, she looked strange, like."

De Luca nodded gravely, biting his cheek. He put a hand in his pocket, settling himself under his trenchcoat, but it wasn't this that was bothering him. He wanted to ask a question and in the end, did so.

"Was there also a red-headed woman?" he asked.

Assuntina nodded. "Signora Valeria was the only one nice to me. But there was a mean one, with black hair."

"Short, with glasses?" De Luca asked. Valeria was back in his thoughts, floating around.

"Yes. Signor Rehinard called her 'Your Excellence' and was always joking around with her, but I once heard them fighting. She was saying: 'Leave my son alone, my son.' She seemed really angry." Assuntina sniffed and wiped her nose with her bare forearm, leaving a lucid trail on her brown flesh. De Luca was about to pull a handkerchief out of his pocket but was so overwhelmed by his thoughts that he forgot what he was doing midway, his fingers only just slipped in his pocket. He nodded two or three times to himself, gaze lost in space, and then came to.

"Listen," he said. "Just one last thing: did Signor Rehinard ever try to . . . did you and he . . .?"

Assuntina gritted her teeth, her eyes and face on fire, and De Luca lifted an arm, shaking his head, because he recognized that look and knew from experience that he wouldn't be getting any more out of that barefooted, disheveled girl sitting on the rock.

"What do you expect, Commissa, they're southerners, peasants." Pugliese blew the dust off the brim of his hat. "They see the police and scare. Assuntina's mother told me that her brother has been watching over her since her fiancé left for Greece in '40 and that he doesn't let anyone get near her. When he's not in prison, I'd like to add, because that Manna is a bad sort, a habitual criminal, quick with his fists and with a knife . . . He got out of jail yesterday. It wouldn't have been a bad idea to bring him with us, given we'd already cuffed him."

"Forget about it, Pugliese, we've got enough trouble as it is." De Luca was sitting in the back, buried in his trench coat as Marcon drove, machine gun on his lap. They were heading back to the station. Tangled up in his overcoat, Pugliese tried to turn around, and moved an arm with difficulty to free himself.

"Did I tell you about Albertini, Commissa? I still haven't heard from him and I'm starting to get worried. He called and said that they were about to arrest him, and had only told him that Littorio Alfieri is second lieutenant and is up at a camp in the mountains at the moment, on the lookout for partisans. But maybe he'd been able to find out some more."

"We need to know more."

"Why?" Pugliese lifted himself up, nearly climbing onto the seat. "The Chief called again, yesterday afternoon, and he told us to continue with the Tedesco lead. Cut it short, he said." Pugliese gestured, moving his flattened hand to and fro.

"Cut it short my ass," De Luca said. He was feeling awful in that moment: he hadn't slept, he hadn't eaten and he felt as if he had a spider's web over his face. If he lowered his eyelids his eyes stung. "Sonia Tedesco is nothing more than a poor, desperate kid, half crazy, and I'm almost certain she doesn't have anything to do with Rehinard's death. First of all, he was her dealer and I don't see why she would've killed him. Then there's that wineglass story. If it's true that . . . " He was about to say, "If it's true that Valeria . . . " but he caught himself. "If it's true that the Suvich woman saw the glass then Sonia had already left. I'm thinking something different now."

"The witch?" asked Pugliese and De Luca looked at him. He had a vague smile on his thin lips, beneath that beak nose, though that was Maresciallo Pugliese's typical expression.

"No," De Luca said. "Maybe, but I don't think so. I mean the professor's wife, the little brunette who was always at Rehinard's place and then argued with him over her son. Why? Christ, what I wouldn't give to interrogate her my way."

"Your way?" said Pugliese and De Luca saw that tight smile again, seeming to mock him. Just then the car stopped abruptly. Pugliese slid forward in his seat, turning around, and Marcon put a hand on the machine gun. De Luca stuck his head out and saw a GNR private gesticulating, telling them to turn around and head off.

"Partisans," said the private when he saw Pugliese's badge. "They're shooting from a roof. You can't get through."

"Let's take via Mastella," Pugliese told Marcon, but De Luca stopped him, putting a hand on his shoulder.

"Wait, I'm not coming to the station, you two go. I'm going to Rosina's, I want to be able to move and phone without being watched. And I want Albertini. And I want Silvia Alfieri." *And I want Valeria*, he thought but didn't say. In front, reflected in the rearview mirror, Pugliese still wore that thin smile of his.

CHAPTER EIGHT

"Hello, Valeria?"
"No, Signora Valeria is not at home. She went out and will be back later. Who is calling?"
"It doesn't matter. Thanks. I'll call back later."

"Italian SS Legion, who's calling? You're looking for who? One minute, I'll put you through to the lieutenant."
"Second Lieutenant De Bosio, who am I speaking to? Commissario De Luca . . . No, there's no Albertini here . . . Yesterday? I don't know, I came on duty today. Wait one moment, please."
"Maresciallo Di Matteo, who's speaking? Commissario Albertini? Who's Albertini? Yes, someone from the station came here yesterday, I spoke with him. He was asking about Lieutenant Alfieri, and then left. No, he left alone, the lieutenant isn't here, he's entitled to a day off . . . they discovered another English airdrop for the rebels, up in the hills. It's the fourth one this month . . . No, I wouldn't know where this Albertini has gone to . . . maybe Massobrio does, one second . . . "
"Corporal Massobrio, at your command. Yes, I saw him. He left with a soldier, but I don't remember who. I think I might have seen them later, in a bar, but I'm not sure. No, out of town, on the outskirts. Should I pass you back to Maresciallo Di Matteo? Hello? Hello?"

"Hello, Valeria?"

"No, signora is not at home. Who is calling?"

"Could you tell me where she went, please?"

"I don't know. Signora Valeria went out and she hasn't come back yet. Who is calling?"

"It doesn't matter. Don't worry, it doesn't matter."

"Commissario? I can hardly hear you . . . In this city every phone works except the one at the station. What? No, there's no news of Albertini, but the Chief called. He said we have to persist, because we're moving in the right direction and one must strike while the iron is hot. Old dogs have good noses, that's what the fucking asshole said . . . Oh Christ, I forgot the phones are tapped. And you? What did you say? Interesting this English airdrop thing, Commissa, very interesting, but dangerous. I said, dangerous. Okay, bye then, I'll be waiting for an update. I said, an update! Christ, this fucking phone!"

"Special Guard Anaclerico Antonio speaking, give me the Mobile Squad . . . Brigadier, we've got a dead man here, in via Montanara, they've thrown him in a ditch. He's got papers on him, he's a police officer too. Just a second, I'll take a look . . . yes, here we are, his name's Albertini."

"Hello, Valeria?"

CHAPTER NINE

He was half hidden in the long grass, face down, and from the street one could only see his legs, sticking straight up, over the edge of the ditch, just like a V. His pants had slid down over his ankles, uncovering the white bare skin above his socks, giving the impression, raw and real, that those shoes in the air, in that farcical position, really did belong to a corpse.

De Luca stood by the roadside and looked down, into the ditch. Beside him, Pugliese was making a strange sound, like a hiss, breathing deeply, his eyes red, whereas Marcon was crying outright.

"I was bicycling by and I found him," said Special Guard Anaclerico. "Who knows how long he's been there, but around here nobody ever says anything. He had this on his back, I took it off or else it would've blown away."

He handed a piece of paper to De Luca, who held it tight as it flapped in the warm wind. *Fucking fascist pig* was written on it. De Luca showed it to Pugliese, who glanced at it quickly then turned back to Albertini, stuffed headfirst in the ditch, arms opened crosswise over the flattened grass.

"They shot him in the back of the head, but they weren't partisans," said Pugliese. "Not Albertini."

"Why?" asked De Luca.

"Partisans wouldn't have killed Albertini. Don't ask me to say more, Commissario, please."

De Luca leaned down over the ditch and pushed aside the grass with one hand, so that he could get a better look. Marcon groaned and walked away quickly.

"Poor Albertini," sighed Pugliese. "Without meaning to, he got mixed up in such a dirty business and these days you can get yourself killed even for a lot less. These weren't Tedesco's men, Commissario, or else they'd have killed you, not him."

De Luca nodded. "Right."

"And now, if we go down to the Italian SS Legion asking questions without the Chief's backing they'll end up arresting and killing us as well."

"Right."

"What a shitty job. So, what to do?"

It wasn't a rhetorical question, even though they both knew the answer. But it was an answer that had to come from De Luca.

"Let's go to Alfieri's house. I'd say it's time to meet the family, this Littorio and his mother. We've even waited too long."

"But the Chief wants us to get Sonia Tedesco. He even called—"

De Luca stood up, with a sinister crack in his knees that made him waver.

"I don't care a damn about the Chief," he said firmly, making for the car.

"Stay here, and don't let anybody in. Got it?"

Marcon nodded, leaning against the wall alongside the front door and De Luca rang the bell. They waited only a few seconds.

"Yes?"

"Urgent message from the Party. Open up, please."

The door opened and De Luca rushed inside, pushing aside an old maid who began wheezing with fear.

"Police! Who's home?"

"There's Signora Alfieri, but you . . . but you . . . "

"Littorio Alfieri, where is he?"

"Master Littorio isn't here, he's out . . . "

"Where is Signora Alfieri?"

The woman lifted her hand and pointed to a square court-yard with a staircase, behind a small iron gate left open, that led upstairs. Pugliese took her by the arm, forcing her to follow him, behind De Luca who was already crossing the court-yard. They went up the stairs under a vaulted hall, in which the muffled sound of a radio echoed, and stopped in front of a door, where Pugliese pushed the woman against the wall and put his hand in his pocket, on the gun. The radio was playing that hit *But oh the legs, oh the legs, I like them the best . . .*

De Luca opened the door without knocking and went in. Silvia Alfieri looked at him amazed, mouth agape.

She was just as the descriptions had her: minute, specta-cles, long straight black hair. She had a slender face, with quite an intelligent look, mobile and nervous like her hands with their long fingernails and her eyes, small, and bright even behind the glasses. She was kneeling on the floor, on a rug, burning some papers in the fireplace.

"Are you that cold?" De Luca asked.

"And who are you?"

"Police, Commissario De Luca. I have a few questions to ask you."

"Get out of my house at once."

Dark eyes may be nice, and blue eyes beguile . . .

De Luca went near to the fireplace and, using the toe of his shoe, edged a piece of singed paper that had slipped onto the rug back into the fire.

"I need some explanations from you," he said. "A lot of explanations." He held out his hand to help her up but she ignored him. She stood up in front of him, smoothing her skirt over her legs, throwing her head back to look at him, as she was much shorter. De Luca tried to imagine her striking Rehinard, first in the chest, then . . .

"Is your husband out?"

"My husband is in Milan with Il Duce and when he learns of this intrusion . . . He is waiting for me and I am in quite a hurry. So, if you don't mind, I must ask you to leave."

Two darling little hands that know how to caress . . .

De Luca sat in an armchair, turning his back to the fire that was starting to make him hot, and Silvia turned nervously towards the door, where Pugliese and the maid were watching in silence.

"Gianna!" she said with a shrill note in her voice. "Go and phone the police immediately and ask for the Chief."

De Luca sighed calmly. "You're in a hurry to leave?" he said. "And I'm going to arrest you for the murder of Vittorio Rehinard."

Silvia Alfieri's eyes shot open so wide that her lips stretched into a kind of smile.

"You must be insane!"

De Luca shrugged. "Perhaps. But to begin with I'll confiscate your papers and then send you on such a tour of police stations that before the Chief finds you the war might well be over."

But two long legs your heart will not resist . . .

Silvia opened her mouth and tried to say something but only a sigh, disfigured by that tense smile, came out. She turned off the radio, moved towards the door, swiftly on her high-heels, and closed the door in Pugliese's face, then walked over to a table and pulled a cigarette out of a purse. She lit it; the lighter's flame flickered in her glasses.

"Your visit is just what I needed," she said, blowing out smoke. She sat down in an armchair in front of De Luca and leaned forward, placing her elbows on her knees. She appeared unable to stay still, as she continued moving, swaying, though she seemed calmer.

"What do you want to know?"

"You killed Rehinard."

"What is this, a question? It seems the opposite to me. I slept with Vittorio, as did many others. And I liked it." She blew out smoke and De Luca turned his head to avoid it.

"Either you killed him, or it was your son. Littorio was dealing morphine together with Rehinard, he'd get it from the English airdrops and Rehinard would peddle it. They had a quarrel and he killed him. Then he had one of my men killed."

The smile on Silvia's lips grew a little tighter around the white cylinder of the cigarette. She crossed her legs, nervously twisting her ankle.

"Him or you," said De Luca. "Or both."

Silvia stood up and threw the cigarette into the fire. She leaned against the fireplace, turning her back to him, the seam of her stockings in constant movement, like a wave.

"You've haven't understood anything," she said. "And you've understood too much. Littorio has got nothing to do with it, that morning he was on duty, in the hills." She went back to get another cigarette, lighting it immediately. "My husband and his friends are fools," she said. "They think they can make a deal, that they'll be able to carve out a space for themselves for what's later, but everything is going to pieces here, there's no more time and they are too compromised. It makes me laugh, this idiotic rivalry with Tedesco to see who is the cleverest and most available collaborator . . . Collaborate! As soon as the front falls they'll chase them down and put them all up against a wall without even asking their names."

She laughed, and De Luca shifted uncomfortably in the armchair for her words annoyed him. He gestured for her to continue.

"Littorio and I wanted to get to Switzerland, at once, but you need money. This is why we went into business with Rehinard. Littorio sold him the morphine, and Rehinard was always in need, for his trafficking: he supplied every respectable family in the city."

De Luca crossed his arms over his chest leaning against the backrest. That, at least, was one stable fact.

"Where is Littorio now?"

She puffed cigarette smoke in the air, and dispersed it with a hand.

"Vanished, flown away. He deserted this morning and has gone over to the partisans."

"Why did you argue with Rehinard?"

Silvia shrugged. She could have told him anything, but by that point she was talking and couldn't stop herself, trembling with tension.

"I hated him, but he had such a way about him, and then, he was so handsome that I always went back. I knew he was a bastard, and that he slept with every woman, but I didn't care, ours was a deal between equals: my husband's influence for his abilities. But then I arranged for him to meet Littorio, and he took my son to bed too. What a bastard!" Silvia Alfieri shook her head, clenching her teeth. She threw this cigarette into the fire too. "When I went to him that day it was to end the morphine affair, because there wasn't much time left and we wanted to leave. Instead I found him on the floor. I didn't kill him, even though I would have willingly, because he was already dead."

"That you have to prove," said De Luca, but he felt uneasy, something was troubling him. Silvia pointed to the fireplace, the papers on the rug and the packed bags.

"Isn't this enough for you?" she said with that smile. "Do you really think I'm stupid enough to wring the neck of the goose that lays the golden eggs? Without that episode, by now I'd be in Switzerland with Littorio instead of burning papers in the fireplace."

That was exactly what was worrying De Luca, who all of a sudden felt exhausted. He passed his hand over his face, roasted by that fire, absurd at the end of April, while he tried to steady and put aside a series of thoughts that were tormenting him, unrelenting, en masse.

"Is this why also the porter and his wife are dead? Because they saw you coming out of Rehinard's before finding him dead?"

"The porter called me that same morning and wanted to blackmail me, the fool. But I told my husband everything. I didn't know they were dead and frankly I couldn't care less." Silvia shrugged and gazed at him scornfully. "Are you satisfied now?" she said. Then she kneeled on the rug and started burning papers again as if he had never even entered the room, so De Luca got up, switched the radio back on, and left the room in silence.

They didn't say anything until the station. Pugliese was driving in silence, absorbed, as if he was listening to the engine, and beneath the brim of his hat, Marcon wore his typical impenetrable look. De Luca wasn't in the mood for talking. He clenched his teeth, trembling with a cold anger that was making his muscles hurt, like a fever. He felt the need to move, to do something, to do anything, but, disoriented by a series of thoughts crowding his mind, all together, irritating, he didn't know what.

When he stopped in front of the station's gray building Pugliese shut off the engine, and turned around.

"I'll ask you again: what do we do?"

De Luca shrugged—a rapid, rigid movement that hurt his neck—but then shook his head, pressing his lips together tight in a mean look.

"Oh no, for God's sake," he muttered. "We can't get Albertini's and Galimberti's killers anymore, but I want whoever killed Rehinard. Because it might not interest anyone, but it does interest me."

Marcon said something, pointing through the window, but De Luca was so caught up in his thoughts he didn't hear him and Pugliese looked at De Luca, one eyebrow raised in a curious look.

"We've been tools in a political struggle and have stumbled onto a drug trade that we can't touch anymore," said De Luca. "But Rehinard is another story. There's still a lot to do: we could ask for a second post-mortem examination and search warrants and have them all tailed, but seriously, this time . . . "

Marcon came back to the car carrying a newspaper that he passed to Pugliese through the side window.

"And there are still people to hear, to put under . . . There are informers to check out, and there's that damned paper knife that can't be found."

"We've solved the case, Commissario."

De Luca stopped, mouth open, and lifted his eyes to Pugliese.

"The case? Who says so?"

"The newspaper says, special evening edition. We've been terrific, all in three days."

Pugliese threw the newspaper on the backseat and De Luca looked at it, without understanding. At first he only make out a white, indistinct but strangely familiar blotch, but when he managed to focus he realized there were two bodies on a bed, lying on a sheet, white, exactly. He understood that it was Sonia Tedesco only when he read the headline.

But what does it mean? he asked himself. "What does it mean?" he said aloud.

"It means," said Pugliese, reading together with De Luca

from over his shoulder, "that little Sonia and her boyfriend, *under the close surveillance of the brilliant Commissario De Luca,* killed themselves with poison this afternoon, thus *demonstrating unequivocally their guilt in the murder* of that son of a bitch Vittorio Rehinard. Congratulations, Commissario, the case is closed. What do you think, have we won a commendation?"

De Luca grabbed the newspaper and threw it out the window furiously. "Why?" he said. "Why did they kill themselves?"

"Maybe because they were desperate. How could they find morphine with half the force on their backs? But the paper doesn't talk about morphine; it talks about orgies, blasphemous rites. I don't think they'll be giving us another postmortem now."

De Luca held his face between his hands, sighing, blowing out through his fingers all the vibrating vigor that anger had filled his body with minutes before. He'd never felt so tired, dulled, and would have liked to turn himself off, like some kind of radio, and only turn himself back on the following day after a night's sleep, his valves cooled.

"The Chief'll want to see you," said Pugliese. "And also Vitali."

"But I don't want to see them." De Luca gestured to Pugliese to get out of the car and got into the driver's seat.

"But what shall I say if they look for you?"

"Tell them I was tired and I went home. I deserve it, don't I? I solved a case in only three days."

De Luca was dreaming of being asleep and woke with a start, for a noise, the metallic sound of a door closing, tore him painfully from his uncomfortable drowse. He opened his eyes in the dull light, for an instant asking himself where he was; the colored glass door reminded him that he was in the waiting room of Valeria's apartment, seated on the sofa, where he had fallen asleep, his head resting on his arm. A movement behind the glass, an indistinct shadow, told him that somebody had just entered.

"Valeria," De Luca called, moving his numb arm. She passed in front of him indifferently, turning her back to him while disappearing into a room. He followed her and stopped at the door because it was the bedroom and she was unbuttoning her suit jacket.

"The door was open," De Luca said to the indifferent shoulders. "I was waiting for you and I fell asleep. It must be late."

"It's almost morning," Valeria said, without turning. She dropped her jacket onto the bed and began unbuttoning her blouse, but stopped immediately.

"I'm very tired," she said. "And would like to go to bed. Would you mind leaving, please?"

"I'd like to talk to you," De Luca said, realizing he had almost whined the words.

"I don't want to talk to you. I don't want to see you ever again." Valeria went back to opening her blouse. From behind, De Luca could only see her shoulders moving and her white neck, bare, for her red hair had been pulled up. She lifted and lowered herself on her heels, slipping her shoes off.

"Are you still here?" she said.

De Luca didn't say anything. The windows were closed and the room was nearly dark, with a gray, heavy half-light that had filled him with the absurd desire to throw himself on the bed, like that bunched-up jacket, curl up like a fetus and sleep for at least a hundred thousand years. Instead, he took a step forward, clenching his teeth with all the force of the mute anger that was flooding him, and with a stiff and sharp movement, he swept clear the top of a bureau, knocking everything to the floor. Valeria sprang around with a frightened look.

"You're crazy!"

"Maybe," said De Luca. "Or maybe I'm just tired."

"Go home then. Or go back to the station to pick up another medal."

"You're a fool."

"And you're a murderer," murmured Valeria, and he suddenly slapped her, a quick, sharp blow with the back of his hand that made her turn her head to one shoulder. The gesture drained out all his anger and De Luca felt empty and ridiculous, his arm motionless at his side, fingers stinging. Valeria remained with her head turned aside, breathing heavily though half-closed lips, breast heaving beneath her open blouse.

"You might as well have killed Sonia yourself," she said. "And that other wretch."

"Many people have died in this story," De Luca said.

"Yes, and for what? For a bastard like Rehinard? How disgusting. But now your case is solved, isn't it? You'll have to find something else to get your mind off the rationing."

De Luca shook his head. "Nothing is solved," he said. "I have a lot of questions for you."

"I don't want to tell you anything."

"You have to."

"Why? What'll you do to me? Tie me to a chair and burn me with a cigarette, like you did in the old days?"

"I never did that!" De Luca cried, clenching his fists. "It wasn't me who did certain things. I just did my job. I'm a cop, that's all!"

Valeria looked at him, smiling. There was a cruel look in her eyes partially covered by a lock of red hair that had slipped over her brow when De Luca hit her. She really did look like a witch.

"Go tell the partisans," she whispered.

De Luca sat on the bed, leaning his arms on his knees. He sighed, exhausted.

"As far as we know, there were three of you that morning," said De Luca stubbornly. "In Rehinard's apartment. First Sonia, and last Silvia Alfieri, but Rehinard was already dead. You could have killed him."

Valeria didn't reply. She just gazed at him with that intolerable light in her red eyes and that ironic, inscrutable curl on her lips. De Luca lifted his eyes to her—ruffled witch ready for bed—her blouse open, and her skirt partly unbuttoned. He reached out and took her by the wrist, pulling her towards him.

"Give me at least one reason," he said, while she sought to regain her balance and not fall on him. "Give me one reason why it couldn't have been you."

Valeria pulled back, violently jerking her arm free. "You give me a reason," she screamed. "Why should it have been me? You tell me why, it's your job! I was completely indifferent to Rehinard. And I didn't hate him, because he didn't even deserve that. I only cared if he was dead or alive when I went to him, because what he could do nobody else knew how to do!"

De Luca lowered his eyes, blushing without wanting to. She finished unbuttoning her skirt and then stepped out of the ring of fabric that had fallen to the floor. She began to prepare the bed as if he weren't there.

"Where were you last night?" De Luca asked, avoiding looking at her, feeling her perfume near and the swish of her skirt. He would've liked to reach out and touch her, caress her, but no longer had the courage.

"I've been out," she said. "But I didn't kill anyone this time. But if you want, you can arrest me for procuring an abortion."

De Luca lifted his head; bent over folding the sheets, she looked at him from over a shoulder.

"Don't worry," she said disdainfully. "It wasn't for me. It

was a young girl whose boyfriend had gotten her in trouble."
She smiled and, shaking her head, went back to arranging her
pillow. "Quite a coincidence, she was the maid of your friend
Rehinard."

De Luca stiffened, as a shudder sent its cold wave through
him making his skin crawl.

"Assuntina?" he said in a hoarse voice.

"Yes, Assuntina. I was like an aunt to her too. The Germans picked up her boyfriend a few days ago. She wanted a
doctor, and I went with her."

"Her boyfriend has been at the front for the past four
years," De Luca murmured. Valeria stopped making the bed
and turned towards him, her face tensing.

"No," she said. "Please no."

De Luca jumped to his feet, shook his fist in the air, tight-
lipped, and struck his forehead, hard.

"What a fool!" he said through his teeth. "God, what a fool
I am!"

He took a step towards the door. She tried to grab him by
the arm, brushing her fingers against his trench coat, without
managing to stop him.

"Where are you going?" she said. "What do you want to
do?" But he didn't seem to hear her, shaking his head and
continuing to mutter "What a fool" to himself, like an idiot.
She watched him leave, then tried to run after him, barefoot
and in her underwear, to the stairs, but it was too late and all
she heard was the building door close.

CHAPTER TEN

They caught her that same morning while she was waiting in line for bread outside the only open bakery. When she saw them getting close, serious and determined, from three different directions, Assuntina knew immediately what they were after and didn't even try to escape. She remained motionless, and only looked around with a helpless look when they took her by the arms, one from each side, and Pugliese quickly handcuffed her. Then they took her over to the car where De Luca was waiting, leaning against the door with his arms crossed over his chest.

That morning she had gone to Rehinard's house to tell him that she was pregnant. She had found out on the very same day he had fired her, but she'd hesitated, not knowing what to do, without telling anyone because her brother would have killed her the minute he got out of jail. Only the porter had seen her, while she was going up, and Rehinard had gotten angry because it was very early, but he had let her in, without saying a word. She had behaved as usual, she had cleaned everything and made his bed, for she wanted to show him how things would be if he decided to keep her; she tried to speak to him, but all those women arrived, that strange blonde and her friend Valeria, and she'd hidden in the bedroom. Only at the end, with difficulty, because she was ashamed, had she been able to tell him that she was expecting his child. Rehinard hadn't gotten angry, as she expected, hadn't taken her in his arms, as she hoped, hadn't even sent her away. He had only began to laugh, just laugh, and every time he looked at her he laughed even more, it seemed like he never wanted to stop. So she'd picked up the paper knife that was on the desk and hit him straight in the heart, like her brother had taught her once, under and up, pushing hard on the blade and when he'd fallen, she had hit him again, with all the anger that was driving her and had made her stony and heartless, hard as rock. Then she'd left, leaving the door open, and had returned home. Only after a while she'd become aware of the paper knife still in her hand, in her bloodied fist; so she'd thrown it away, like an idiot, in the main entrance of a building that she indicated, and indeed, when they went to get it, they found it right there, on the floor of the entrance, dried blood on the blade. Nobody at home knew anything, not her mother, not even her brother, who had nothing to do with it, and, this said, Assuntina stopped talking, shut her lips tight, one against the other, and she wouldn't have said anything more, even under torture. But it was already enough.

"It was that simple!" said De Luca gaily, sitting in the front seat. "The crime of a poor, jealous and slighted maid! But when there's someone like Rehinard involved, with his traffic, everything gets complicated and all kinds of possibilities arise. If Rehinard hadn't been what he was, we'd have solved the case immediately."

"A lot of people wouldn't have been killed," said Pugliese darkly, sitting in the back next to Assuntina, dumb and deaf, handcuffs around her thin wrists. De Luca wasn't listening to him. He was euphoric, and was even feeling hungry.

"I can't wait to shove her right under the Chief's nose," he said, pleased. "A self-confessed offender! Talk about absurd hypotheses! I really want to see their faces, his and that other son of a bitch, Vitali."

"What are we going to do, Commissa, are we really going to take her in?" asked Pugliese. De Luca turned and looked at him from over his shoulder.

"What kind of question is that, Maresciallo?" he said calmly. "Of course we're going to take her in, she's a murderer. I can't let her go, Pugliese, I'm a policeman."

Pugliese sighed and De Luca glanced quickly at Assuntina, her chin high and gaze fixed, then went back to looking out the window, thinking again about the Chief and about what he was going to say to him. He felt so satisfied and relaxed that he thought maybe he might even call Valeria, explain himself, clarify, perhaps even apologize. He noticed something unusual out on the street, which, for a moment, lost in thought, he wasn't able to figure out, but then, looking closer, managed to see what it was.

"How come the shops are closed at this hour?" he asked, and Pugliese looked outside too. They saw a GNR truck loaded with soldiers passing, and instead of stopping to make the shops reopen, it drove straight ahead.

"Strange," said Pugliese. A car passed them, honking, then a second later halted, screeching the brakes, and reversed back, blocking their way. Captain Rassetto got out of the car but remained on the running board, hanging off the door.

"De Luca," he yelled. "Don't be an idiot, De Luca, come away with us!"

De Luca leaned out of the window, surprised and a little worried.

"Come with you?" he said. "But I'm on my way to the station. I've just solved this case and the Chief—"

"Don't be an idiot, De Luca," Rassetto repeated. "The Allies crossed the river Po this morning, we're all moving north. Your Chief'll be in Milan by now, if he hasn't already reached Switzerland."

De Luca moved back in the car. A sudden fear had dried his tongue and he merely stuttered, swallowing before speaking.

"I . . . I've got nothing to do with them," he said. "I made an arrest, and I have to go to the station . . . That's my place, I'm a policeman."

He turned to look at Pugliese, who watched him without a smile, without saying a word, his small, narrow eyes above his beak nose, his head oily with grease, and his hat on his knees.

"Pugliese," De Luca said. "You *know* . . . I know you know. What will happen if I . . . What will happen to me if I stay?"

Pugliese didn't move, he only puckered his lips a little. De Luca had never seen him with such a grave look.

"Better if you go too, Commissa," he said quietly, almost in a whisper. "It'd be better."

De Luca dropped his gaze and ran a hand over his face, biting his lip. The driver of Rassetto's car blew the horn twice.

"Better if I go," De Luca repeated. "Yes, better if I go." He opened the door and put a leg out, but Pugliese lifted himself from the seat and taking him by an arm, stopped him. He held out his open hand.

"I'm sorry, Commissario. Good luck."

De Luca shook the hand, with a quick nod of the head, then got out and ran to the waiting car, engine running and door open, that, without giving him time to close it, sped off, heading north.

ABOUT THE AUTHOR

Carlo Lucarelli is one of Italy's best-loved crime writers. He was born in Parma in 1960. His publishing debut came with the extremely successful "De Luca Trilogy" in 1990 and he has since published over a dozen novels and collections of stories. He is an active member of several Italian and international writer's association, he teaches at Alessandro Baricco's Holden School in Turin and in Padua's maximum-security prison. Several of his novels have been translated into French for Gallimard's renowned "Noir" series. He conducts the program "Blue Night" on Italian network television, and his novels *Almost Blue* and *Lupo Mannaro* have both been made into successful films.

The Days of Abandonment

Elena Ferrante

Fiction - 192 pp - $14.95 - isbn 1-933372-00-1

"Stunning . . . The raging, torrential voice of the author is something rare."—Janet Maslin, *The New York Times*

"I could not put this novel down. Elena Ferrante will blow you away."—Alice Sebold, author of *The Lovely Bones*

Rarely have the foundations upon which our ideas of motherhood and womanhood rest been so candidly questioned. This compelling novel tells the story of one woman's headlong descent into what she calls an "absence of sense" after being abandoned by her husband. Olga's "days of abandonment" become a desperate, dangerous freefall into the darkest places of the soul as she roams the empty streets of a city that she has never learned to love. When she finds herself trapped inside the four walls of her apartment in the middle of a summer heat wave, Olga is forced to confront her ghosts, the potential loss of her own identity, and the possibility that life may never return to normal again.

Cooking with Fernet Branca

James Hamilton-Paterson
Fiction - 288 pp - $14.95 - isbn 1-933372-01-X

"A work of comic genius."—*The Independent*

Gerald Samper, an effete English snob, has his own private hilltop
in Tuscany where he wiles away his time working as a ghostwriter
for celebrities and inventing wholly original culinary
concoctions—including ice-cream made with garlic and the bitter,
herb-based liqueur of the book's title. Gerald's idyll is shattered by
the arrival of Marta, on the run from a crime-riddled former soviet
republic. A series of hilarious misunderstands brings this odd couple into ever closer and more disastrous proximity.

Minotaur
Benjamin Tammuz
Fiction/Mystery - 192 pp - $14.95 - isbn 1-933372-02-8

"A novel about the expectations and compromises that humans create for themselves . . . Very much in the manner of William Faulkner and Lawrence Durrell."—*The New York Times*

An Israeli secret agent falls hopelessly in love with a young English girl. Using his network of shady contacts and his professional expertise, he takes control of her life without ever revealing his identity. *Minotaur* is a complex and utterly original story about a solitary man driven from one side of Europe to the other by his obsession.

www.europaeditions.com

Total Chaos
Jean-Claude Izzo
Fiction/Mystery - 256 pp - $14.95 - isbn 1-933372-04-4

"Jean-Claude Izzo's growing literary renown and huge sales are leading to a recognizable new trend in continental fiction: the rise of the sophisticated Mediterranean thriller . . . Caught between pride and crime, racism and fraternity, tragedy and light, messy urbanization and generous beauty, the city for Montale is a Utopia, an ultimate port of call for exiles. There, he is torn between fatalism and revolt, despair and sensualism."—*The Economist*

This first installment in the legendary *Marseilles Trilogy* sees Fabio Montale turning his back on a police force marred by corruption and racism and taking the fight against the mafia into his own hands.

The Big Question
Wolf Erlbruch
Children's Illustrated Fiction - 52 pp - $14.95 - isbn 1-933372-03-6

Named Best Book at the 2004 Children's Book Fair in
Bologna.

A stunningly beautiful and poetic illustrated book for children that
poses the biggest of all the big questions: why am I here? A chorus
of voices—including the cat's, the baker's, the pilot's and the soldier's—offers us some answers. But nothing is certain, except that
as we grow each one of us will pose the question differently and be
privy to different answers.

www.europaeditions.com

The Butterfly Workshop

Wolf Erlbruch

Children's Illustrated Fiction - 40 pp - $14.95 - isbn 1-933372-12-5

For children and adults alike . . . Odair, one of the "Designers of All Things" and grandson of the esteemed inventor of the rainbow, has been banished to the insect laboratory as punishment for his overactive imagination. But he still dreams of one day creating a cross between a bird and a flower. Then, after a helpful chat with a dog . . .

The Goodbye Kiss
Massimo Carlotto
Fiction/Mystery - 192 pp - $14.95 - isbn 1-933372-05-2

"The best living Italian crime writer."—*Il Manifesto*

An unscrupulous womanizer, as devoid of morals now as he once was full of idealistic fervor, returns to Italy where he is wanted for a series of crimes. To avoid prison he sells out his old friends, turns his back on his former ideals, and cuts deals with crooked cops. To earn himself the guise of respectability he is willing to go even further, maybe even as far as murder.

www.europaeditions.com

Hangover Square
Patrick Hamilton
Fiction/Mystery - 280 pp - $14.95 - isbn 1-933372-06-0

"Hamilton is a sort of urban Thomas Hardy: always a pleasure to read, and as social historian he is unparalleled."—Nick Hornby

Adrift in the grimy pubs of London at the outbreak of World War II, George Harvey Bone is hopelessly infatuated with Netta, a cold, contemptuous, small-time actress. George also suffers from occasional blackouts. During these moments one thing is horribly clear: he must murder Netta.

I Loved You for Your Voice

Sélim Nassib

Fiction - 256 pp - $14.95 - isbn 1-933372-07-9

"Om Kalthoum is great. She really is."—Bob Dylan

Love, desire, and song set against the colorful backdrop of modern Egypt. The story of the Arab world's greatest and most popular singer, Om Kalthoum, told through the eyes of the poet Ahmad Rami, who wrote her lyrics and loved her in vain all his life. Spanning over five decades in the history of modern Egypt, this passionate tale of love and longing provides a key to understanding the soul, the aspirations and the disappointments of the Arab world.

Love Burns

Edna Mazya

Fiction/Mystery - 192 pp - $14.95 - isbn 1-933372-08-7

"Starts out as a psychological drama and becomes a strange, funny, unexpected hybrid: a farce thriller. A great book."—*Ma'ariv*

Ilan, a middle-aged professor of astrophysics, discovers that his young wife is having an affair. Terrified of losing her, he decides to confront her lover instead. Their meeting ends in the latter's murder—the unlikely murder weapon being Ilan's pipe—and in desperation, Ilan disposes of the body in the fresh grave of his kindergarten teacher. But when the body is discovered . . .

www.europaeditions.com

Departure Lounge
Chad Taylor
Fiction/Mystery - 176 pp - $14.95 - isbn 1-933372-09-5

"Entropy noir . . . The hypnotic pull lies in the zigzag dance of its forlorn characters, casting a murky, uneasy sense of doom."—*The Guardian*

A young woman mysteriously disappears. The lives of those she has left behind—family, acquaintances, and strangers intrigued by her disappearance—intersect to form a captivating latticework of coincidences and surprising twists of fate. Urban noir at its stylish and intelligent best.

The Jasmine Isle
Ioanna Karystiani
Fiction - 176 pp - $14.95 - isbn 1-933372-10-9

A modern love story with the force of an ancient Greek tragedy. Set on the spectacular Cycladic island of Andros, *The Jasmine Isle*, one of the finest literary achievements in contemporary Greek literature, recounts the story of the old sea wolf, Spyros Maltambès, and the beautiful Orsa Saltaferos, sentenced to marry a man she doesn't love and to watch while the man she does love is wed to another.

Boot Tracks
Matthew F. Jones
Fiction/Mystery - 208 pp - $14.95 - isbn 1-933372-11-7

"Mr. Jones has created a powerful blend of love and violence, of the grotesque and the tender."—*The New York Times*

Charlie Rankin has recently been released from prison, but prison has not released its grip on him. He owes his life to "The Buddha," who has given him a job to do on the outside: he must kill a man, a man who has done him no harm, a man he has never met. Along the road to this brutal encounter, Rankin meets Florence, who may be an angel in disguise or simply a lonely ex porn star seeking salvation. Together they careen towards their fate, taking the reader along for the ride. A commanding, stylishly written novel that tells the harrowing story of an assassination gone terribly wrong and the man and woman who are taking their last chance to find a safe place in a hostile world.

Dog Day
Alicia Giménez-Bartlett
Fiction/Mystery - 208 pp - $14.95 - isbn 1-933372-14-1

"Giménez-Bartlett has discovered a world full of dark corners and hidden elements."—*ABC*

In this hardboiled fiction for dog lovers and lovers of dog mysteries, detective Petra Delicado and her maladroit sidekick, Garzón, investigate the murder of a tramp whose only friend is a mongrel dog named "Fright." One murder leads to another and Delicado finds herself involved in the sordid, dangerous world of fight dogs. *Dog Day* is first-rate entertainment.

Old Filth
Jane Gardam
Fiction - 256 pp - $14.95 - isbn 1-933372-13-3

"Jane Gardam's beautiful, vivid and defiantly funny novel is a must."—*The Times*

Sir Edward Feathers has progressed from struggling young barrister to wealthy expatriate lawyer to distinguished retired judge, living out his last days in comfortable seclusion in Dorset. The engrossing and moving account of his life, from birth in colonial Malaya, to Wales, where he is sent as a "Raj orphan," to Oxford, his career and marriage, parallels much of the 20th century's dramatic history.

Troubling Love
Elena Ferrante
Fiction - 144 pp - $14.95 - isbn 1-933372-16-8

"Elena Ferrante will blow you away."—Alice Sebold, author of *The Lovely Bones*

Following her mother's untimely and mysterious death, Delia embarks on a voyage of discovery through the streets of her native Naples in search of the truth about her family.

Chourmo
Jean-Claude Izzo
Fiction/Mystery - 256 pp - $14.95 - isbn 1-933372-17-6

"Like the best noir writers—and he is among the best—Izzo not only has a keen eye for detail but also digs deep into what makes men weep."—*Time Out, New York*

The second installment in the legendary *Marseilles Trilogy*.

Death's Dark Abyss
Massimo Carlotto
Fiction/Mystery - 192 pp - $14.95 - isbn 1-933372-18-4

"A narrative voice that is cold, heartless, but, in a creepy way, fascinating."—*The New York Times*

A riveting drama of guilt, revenge, and justice, Massimo Carlotto's *Death's Dark Abyss* tells the story of two men and the savage crime that binds them.

Amazing Disgrace
James Hamilton-Paterson
Fiction - 320 pp - $14.95 - isbn 1-933372-19-2

"Imagine a British John Waters crossed with David Sedaris."
—*The New York Times Book Review*

This hilarious sequel to the popular *Cooking with Fernet Branca* is further evidence of Hamilton-Paterson's wit and comic inventiveness.

Margherita Dolce Vita
Stefano Benni
Fiction - 208 pp - $14.95 - isbn 1-933372-20-6

"A master of political satire infused with a dose of the fantastical."
—*World Literature Today*

Stefano Benni's enormously popular and distinctive mix of the absurd and the satirical has made him one of Italy's most important and best-loved novelists.

One Day A Year
Christa Wolf
Memoir - 650 pp - $14.95 - isbn 1-933372-22-2

"The rewards of reading Christa Wolf can be very considerable."
—*The Times Literary Supplement*

Forty intimate essays written over the course of forty years, on the same day of the year, by one of the 20th century's most important authors.